TAMING ADAM

BURLAP AND BARBED WIRE #2

SHIRLEY PENICK

To my sister Judy, who put up with debilitating headaches for thirty years. I am so happy the doctor finally found the cause and you have your life back. Let's party!

Photography by Jean Woodfin
Cover models: Deanna Ruge and Wade Hayes
Cover design by Cassy Roop of Pink Ink Designs
Editing by Carol Tietsworth

Contact Shirley

www.shirleypenick.com
www.facebook.com/ShirleyPenickAuthor
To sign up for Shirley's New Release Newsletter, send email to shirleypenick@outlook.com, subject newsletter.

ALSO BY SHIRLEY PENICK

Previous books by Shirley Penick

LAKE CHELAN SERIES

The Rancher's Lady: A Lake Chelan novella

Hank and Ellen's story

Sawdust and Satin: Lake Chelan #1

Chris and Barbara's story

Designs on Her: Lake Chelan #2

Nolan and Kristen's story

Smokin': Lake Chelan #3

Jeremy and Amber's story

Coming Soon! Fire on the Mountain: Lake Chelan #4

Trey and Mary Ann's story

BURLAP AND BARBED WIRE SERIES

A Cowboy for Alyssa: Burlap and Barbed Wire #1

Beau and Alyssa's story

Taming Adam: Burlap and Barbed Wire #2

Adam and Rachel's story

Coming Soon! Tempting Chase: Burlap and Barbed Wire #3

Chase and Katie's story

CHAPTER 1

Rachel Reardon tried not to run over the woman who had come tearing out of the large ranch house, jumped over the cow lying in the front yard and skidded to a stop a mere breath from the Silver Bullet's bumper. Before Rachel could get her car shifted into park, her best friend since kindergarten, Alyssa, was yanking open her door and jumping up and down like a crazy person.

"You're finally here!" her friend shrieked.

"Good lord, Alyssa. You're going to scare every animal within a hundred miles." She laughed, as she unhooked her seat belt and clambered out of her car. "Besides, it's only been four days since your big announcement. It takes two to drive here."

Alyssa grabbed her and hugged the stuffing out of her. Rachel held on tight, she'd missed Alyssa while she had been here in Colorado getting her degree, and especially now since Alyssa wasn't coming back to their small home town in eastern Washington. She would be staying in Colorado and getting married.

Alyssa pulled back and shook her finger at Rachel. "Then you could have been here two days ago."

Rachel grinned, Alyssa had always been the leader in their relationship. Rachel enjoyed letting her lead the charge, while she held back and took pictures documenting their adventures. "Maybe with a little warning, I could have been, but you did not indicate—in any way—when we talked, that you would be getting engaged the very next day."

"I didn't know then." Alyssa widened her eyes. "It was quite a surprise to me, too." She giggled. "Oh, I have so much to tell you, let's grab your crap and I'll show you to the guest room."

Rachel put her hands on her hips. "You better not be calling my camera equipment crap, young lady. It took me nearly a whole day to get it all together. Engagement pictures and graduation pictures need completely different supplies. Staying here for three months to help you plan your wedding took some major finagling and I had to bring all kinds of stuff with me. Plus, your step-mom decided to send half your closet, in case you wanted your pictures in something you hadn't taken with you to college. So, some of the crap—as you call it—is yours."

Alyssa laughed and shook her head sadly. "Believe me I know. I think I spent at least six hours on the phone with her, as she went through *every single thing* in my closet. And my guess is their car will be more than half-filled with more of my stuff when they drive down for graduation."

"You *are* going to live here. So, I totally agree." Rachel put her hands on her hips. "In fact, I think every time someone drives that distance they'll be bringing a carload, or even a truckload of your crap. Let's start carrying. All this stuff is going to take us several trips."

"No, it won't." Alyssa turned towards the house and waved. "I made them wait until I had a chance to hug you."

Out of the house streamed a half dozen of the hottest men Rachel had ever seen. They'd been in on the conference call proposal, but they'd been sitting down around the table and the camera had been primarily on Beau and Alyssa, so Rachel hadn't really gotten a good look at any of them. But up close and personal, they all had amazing good looks from the grandfather and father down to the youngest. Even four-year-old Tony was going to be a lady killer when he grew up.

Apparently, the cow was not the least bit interested in being in the path of the unloading route, since she got up and wandered off. Rachel would have to remember to ask Alyssa if that was Dolly, the pet cow of Alyssa's fiancé, since no one seemed the least bit surprised to have a cow chilling in the front yard.

Alyssa started introducing her to everyone and Rachel could hardly keep up. She got Grandpa K easily and his son and daughter-in-law, Travis and Meg Kipling, were obvious. Little Tony and his mom were good too, but once she got to all the guys she was lost. Alyssa had talked about all of them, so she knew their names—but putting faces to those names—was so not happening right now.

"Whoa, I'm going to need name tags."

One of the twins laughed. "I'm Cade, the good looking one of the family. The rest aren't important." He took her hand and placed it on his arm, then picked up a suitcase in the other hand.

The oldest brother, Adam, she thought, wacked his brother on the back of the head and frowned at her. "Don't be an ass, Cade." Then he marched over and took some of her camera equipment out of the car.

Fearing he would not be careful with her equipment, she disengaged from Cade with an apologetic smile, and went over to Adam. "Some of that's very delicate equipment, you need to be careful with it."

He rolled his eyes and drawled, "Yes ma'am, I'll be sure not to break anything. Don't you worry your little head about it, missy. I have seen a camera before." Then he turned on his heel and headed for the house, ignoring her completely.

She looked at Alyssa, who was directing the family, and caught her eye. Alyssa gave her the I'll-explain-later look and went back to unloading the car.

Rachel thought about going back to Cade and letting him escort her in, but decided she was more concerned with her equipment than she was about flirting. Which sadly enough, always seemed to be the case in her life. She handed him a bag with her tripods and told him she'd catch him later.

ADAM KIPLING CARRIED the cameras into the house and to the guest bedroom that—in his opinion—Alyssa should still be using. But once the engagement had been announced she'd moved down the hall to Beau's room. Adam shook his head, maybe he was a prude or something, but he just flat thought it was kind of tacky for the two of them to be tearing up the sheets together in full knowledge of the family. No one else seemed to have a problem with it, so why it chapped him so badly he couldn't tell. If truth be told it was probably still the age difference between them. A seven-year gap still seemed like a lot, but again no one else seemed to think anything about it.

He supposed his stupid brothers were going to be falling all over Rachel, as Cade had already glommed onto her. She was another sexy woman, just like Alyssa, so he couldn't really blame Cade. Rachel was average height for a woman with a petite build and long, wavy, brown hair. She had huge hazel eyes and a great smile that turned up at the corners. A beautiful package. He wasn't sure he wanted to watch a second brother make an ass out of himself. Not his call, though.

He set the camera and equipment cases on the dresser since the desk was about the size of a postage stamp. Why they had such a tiny desk in here he wasn't sure, maybe he should look around and see if they had something larger. Since Rachel was going to be taking and processing a lot of photos over the next couple of months, she would need somewhere to put a laptop, all her camera equipment, memory cards, and other paraphernalia.

Cade came into the room with a suitcase and a tripod bag and started to dump it all on the bed.

Adam shook his head. "No, don't put everything on the bed. Put the suitcase over by the closet and the tripod bag next to the dresser. We need to get Rachel a table or decent sized desk, that one's ridiculous."

Cade looked at the desk and barked out a laugh. "Yeah, you're right, I never noticed. No wonder Alyssa moved in with Beau. He has a nice desk she'll actually be able to *use* for her final report before graduation."

That sealed it, Rachel needed a decent desk. Immediately. He didn't want her to move in with one of his brothers just so she would have a decent workspace. He stayed in the room and directed the rest of the family on where to put all of Rachel's stuff while he looked on his phone for a place to purchase a better desk. He was the money guy in the family, so he knew they could buy one easily enough.

When Rachel and Alyssa came in with the last few things, he had already found a desk that could be here in three days. He frowned at the girls. "I ordered you a bigger desk, so you'll have something to use besides that ridiculous thing under the window. It will be here in three days."

Rachel looked at the desk, then back at him and crossed

her arms. "While I will need something larger and I appreciate you getting me one, that *ridiculous thing under the window* is an antique. It looks like mahogany and it's clearly from the Victorian era, a lady's writing desk, even though the chair doesn't match. How this lovely little desk ended up in the middle of the Colorado mountains would likely be a great tale." She walked over to the tiny table and ran her hands lovingly over the top. Looking around the room she said, "There's enough space in here for both—I think—if you don't mind me keeping it."

He nodded. "Not at all, saves me from having to find somewhere else to stick it." He turned to walk out the door and then remembered his manners, so he tipped his hat at them. "Ladies."

He didn't understand women, he was trying to be helpful and she'd treated him like he was a moron. Well, he probably was when it came to frou-frou antique desks, but still, showing a little appreciation wouldn't hurt her.

RACHEL WAS happy to see all her things so neatly organized, she'd thought it would all be piled on the bed. "Wow, look how nicely they put all my stuff."

Alyssa put her hands on her hips. "Must be Adam's doing. All my belongings were in a huge pile on that bed and I didn't have nearly as much as you do. Adam didn't help with the carrying in when I came, he was busy with Meg and Travis."

Rachel walked over and shut the door then rounded on her friend. "So, what's the deal with him anyway? He seems kind of pissed off that I'm here."

Alyssa sighed and flopped down on the bed. "It's not you, it's me. He thinks I'm too young for Beau or Beau is too old for me. He's been kind of grumpy about it since day one and even told Beau he was making a mistake."

"Well who died and made him sheriff? Beau and you are both adults and seven years isn't all that much. I guess it is while still in public school, but once everyone hits twenty-one it becomes a moot point. What a jerk. Did you guys tell him to butt out and mind his own damn business?" She was so pissed that anyone would rain on her best friend's romance, she wanted to go tell Mr. High and Mighty to back the hell off.

"Beau did, but Adam's still the oldest brother so I think it bothers Beau. He tries not to let it show but—"

"Adam is obviously an asshole, and everyone should just ignore him. Everyone else in the family seems thrilled to have you and Beau together."

Alyssa smiled so big, Rachel thought her face might crack. "They are. Everyone has welcomed me into the family with open arms. Meg is calling me her daughter-in-love."

"Aww, that's so sweet." Rachel really liked that sentiment. It was so much better than daughter in law, like you didn't really have any choice, it was the law, and you just had to suck it up and deal with it.

"Little Tony started calling me Aunt Lyssa the moment he understood he wasn't really calling me an insect. Emma had to write it down and show him the different spellings, he's only four, so it's a wonder that he understands spelling already. He first started calling me Aunt-with-a-U Lyssa. But Beau explained that he didn't need to point out that the word had a U in it because he was using it with my name, so no one would be confused and think he was calling me an insect. Tony thought about it for a while and then I guess he decided to believe Beau. It was adorable."

"He's a little cutie, that's for sure. I love that he wanted to help carry in my things. It's a good thing I had that snack bag, and it was mostly empty from the two-day drive, it was perfect for him."

"It was, he loves to help. You should see the mess he makes in the kitchen. His first time 'smashing potatoes' I almost got hit with a flying spud. They were barely edible, but everyone had two helpings and raved about how good they were." Alyssa laughed. "Now let's get you all settled in. I'll unpack your clothes while you futz around with your camera equipment. Although you will have a new desk in three days, instead of that 'silly thing under the window'."

"*Ridiculous* thing under the window. Get it right, Alyssa." They both laughed like loons and started unpacking what needed to be hung up or put away. While Alyssa chattered on about all the things she wanted them to do in the next few weeks, Rachel wondered if Adam would eventually come around or if she was going to have to slap some sense into him.

CHAPTER 2

Adam saddled his horse, Jake. They both needed a good hard run. Adam knew he wouldn't be able to outrun his thoughts. He was still uncertain about Beau marrying Alyssa, it just didn't seem right to him. And now Rachel was here, and she was going to be a distraction to him and probably every other male on the ranch. Adam knew he could ignore it, since she was so young, but what about everyone else?

He wasn't going to worry about that now, at least he could put it aside for a few minutes to give both his horse and himself some exercise. He spent too much time behind a computer or on the phone, sometimes being the business face of the Rockin' K ranch got old. Fresh air and sunshine was just what he needed to clear his mind. His phone was set on silent, everyone could leave a message, and he'd call them back. Later. He'd left his family a note saying where he was going, so they wouldn't worry. All his bases were covered. He finally had an hour to himself.

He led his horse out of the barn and stopped abruptly when he spotted Alyssa and Rachel walking toward him. The two of them together were nice to look at, both dark-haired beauties. Not that he was interested, of course. And no way was he letting them side track him. He swung up onto his horse and tipped his hat to them. "Ladies."

"Oh, Adam, maybe you know. Is it okay if Rachel and I saddle some horses and ride a bit?" Alyssa asked.

"Absolutely, have fun." He turned his horse toward the pasture.

"Which horse should I give her?"

Adam sighed. Any other time he would be happy to help, just not today, he was wound too tight to be of any help. But he turned back. "We've got plenty to choose from, Alyssa, if they are in the barn you can take your pick. You've been here long enough to know their temperament, and you know Rachel's riding skills."

"But..."

Just then Cliff came out of the barn, thank God. "Cliff, will you give Alyssa a hand picking out a horse for Rachel?"

Cliff looked surprised, but nodded. "Will do."

"Great." Turning his horse, he moved away from the three of them as fast as he could. Cliff could handle it, that wasn't something they normally asked him to do, but he certainly was capable. Adam only had an hour before he'd needed to be back, and he didn't want to spend the whole damn time picking out a horse for Rachel.

RACHEL FROWNED as Adam rode away from them. That man had to be the rudest person on the planet. He couldn't take two minutes out of his precious day to help them? Well fine, they didn't need his help anyway. Jerk.

Cliff suggested a pretty chestnut mare after Alyssa told him about Rachel's equestrian experience. She didn't live on a ranch like Alyssa, but she'd spent hours at the Jefferson House growing up and a fair amount of that had been on horses. She'd never competed like Alyssa did, but she'd spent time learning how to barrel race and she even had a trick or two she could do without embarrassing herself.

Once they got the horses saddled, Alyssa asked, "So, what do you want to see first? The cattle, the pasture, the river, or the haying fields?"

"How about the place you were when the blizzard blew through, and you can tell me the story as we ride out there."

Alyssa laughed. "That was just a spring storm, not a blizzard and I was fine. No real story to tell."

"Uh huh. How many years have I known you? There is a story, and you *are* going to tell me. So, get to talking, missy. Or I'll ask the twins since they seem to know everything and have no secrets. Or shame."

Alyssa rolled her eyes. "I suppose it would be better coming from me."

"Yes." They crossed into the birthing pasture, where new mothers and their babies were still being kept closer to the house. The new calves were so darn cute it was hard to concentrate on what Alyssa was saying, but that event had been a turning point in Alyssa's relationship with Beau, and Rachel wanted to hear the real story. Not the glossed-over version that Alyssa had told everyone else.

"So, it was a sunny spring morning, a little chilly but not too cold. I was in the vet truck..."

THE TENSION in Adam's neck was finally starting to loosen. He'd let Jake have his run and then they'd headed over to the river for a nice cool drink. Jake munched on some of the sweet grass that grew next to the Colorado River. Adam skipped a few rocks and a fish jumped out of the water. The sunlight sparkled on the silver and pink scales of the rainbow trout as it leapt in the air and sent a shower of water drops glistening skyward. It splashed as it landed back into the river and Adam laughed in pure joy of the moment.

The rest of the tension drained from his body and he felt himself center. But play time was over and he needed to get back to the house. He still had to brush his horse down before he went back to his computer in time for the video conference call.

He walked toward Jake, who was still happily munching, when a damn drone came out of nowhere and practically whacked him right between the eyes. He batted at it and shouted. Then the darn thing flew right at his horse who'd looked up to see what the commotion was about. When the drone almost beaned his horse, Jake reared up and then took off at a run toward the barn.

Adam whistled at his horse, but the normally well-behaved animal just kept running like the fires of hell nipped at his heels. Well hell, now he had a good long hike ahead of him unless he could get someone to come get him. If he didn't have the call coming up with a half dozen people spread across four time zones, he'd just walk back. It was only a couple of miles, but he didn't really have the luxury of time. He got out his phone and sent a group text.

Adam: Drone scared Jake, he's headed back to the barn, somebody let him in, brush him down. I'm in the North-East pasture and have a video conference call in 15. Need someone to come get me, asap.

After a flurry of texts it was determined Alyssa and Rachel were the closest. The hands with vehicles were mending the fence and it would take them longer to shore up the hole they'd found before they could come get him. The girls could ride together on Alyssa's horse and he could take the one Rachel was on.

Alyssa: On our way!

Adam: Thanks, I'll be walking toward the house.

Alyssa: Not for long.

Alyssa was true to her word. Adam saw the women racing hell-bent for leather in his direction not five minutes later. His heart stopped when they got within a dozen yards of him. They slowed so they were riding in tandem, brought the horses close together and Rachel stood up in her saddle, then stepped over behind Alyssa and sat down still holding the reins of her horse. By the time they had executed that move they were right on top of him. Rachel tossed him the reins, and he climbed on. The stirrups were too short for him, but he didn't have the time to lengthen them, he'd just have to suck it up.

He yelled, "That was the most foolhardy thing I've ever seen. You don't know these horses well enough to attempt something like that. We'll be talking about it later." He swung the horse around and headed back to the house at a dead run. They were going to get a dressing down, about doing stupid stunts on horses they didn't know, but right now he had to get back for the call.

Rachel yelled after him, "You're welcome." She said something after that, but he couldn't tell if it was his name or "asshole".

CHAPTER 3

Rachel adjusted the height of the tripod holding her Canon 80D. She had come out early to take some pictures of the mountains and pasture in the natural morning light. Not that there weren't a ton of people up bustling around. Feeding horses, checking on the cattle. But Alyssa wasn't up or out yet, so that gave Rachel some time to take some pictures for herself. They were planning to meet in two hours to start on the engagement photos. Alyssa wanted the announcements to come out right after graduation.

Alyssa and Beau were going to be getting married in just a couple of months because they wanted to be back from their honeymoon in time to direct the breeding, which would start in early August. They were pushing it back just a week or two to give them a little more time. It was going to be a darn busy few months.

Alyssa planned on Rachel spending most of that time in Colorado to help with everything, beginning with the engagement photos, then graduation photos, wedding planning and going right on through to the wedding. They would be taking a quick trip back to Washington for her bridal shower and bachelorette party and then the whole family would be driving back to Colorado for the wedding. Rachel wouldn't be the official wedding photographer since she couldn't be both the maid of honor and the primary photographer, but she planned to take a lot of the behind the scenes photos.

She snapped a couple of second's worth of pictures, which would give her about a dozen frames to work with of that scene, then she adjusted the shutter speed to take the same view in an overexposed light, she'd already done the underexposed ones. She loved to play around with HDR shots, the high dynamic range of the three light settings made a much richer finished photograph. Sometimes she did photo stacking too, using a lot more pictures for lots of detail, especially on her close ups, but HDR was her favorite. When she was happy with that scene she moved the camera to a different view. She was working with her wide-angle lens and after that she'd switch to telephoto to zoom in on some of the interesting features in the mountains. She didn't have time to go too far, but there was plenty for her to shoot right from the yard.

"Looks like a Canon 80D," Adam said, as he stopped next to her.

"Yes, it is," she replied, not taking her eye from the view finder. She was still ticked at him for being a jerk yesterday.

"Nice camera."

"I like it, still saving up for a Mark IV."

"Also, a nice camera. Perfect for a professional. Alyssa says you're getting there and even selling some things in an art gallery."

Fine, he was making small talk, she could do that. Rachel finally turned to look at him. "Alyssa is my biggest fan, but yes, I've got people buying my photos, so I can't complain.

She had to drag me into the art gallery, at first, but it's worked out well."

"I can see her doing that, she's certainly a force of nature." He chuckled.

She frowned at him. "I thought you didn't like her."

"Oh no, nothing like that, I think she's a very nice girl. I just don't know if she's mature enough for Beau. He's a very serious vet."

"I don't really think it's your call." She said folding her arms over her chest. Rachel didn't like his presumptuous attitude. "She's serious about working with animals too, did you see any lack of maturity during her internship?"

He kicked at the dirt as he looked out toward the mountains. "No. Actually, quite the opposite. She did an excellent job."

"Then maybe she and Beau know what they're doing." She arched an eyebrow at him.

"I sincerely hope so." He shrugged. "She said you were thinking about art school."

Changing the subject, she would let him off the hook this time, but he better back off or she would really give him a piece of her mind. "I am, but I haven't decided. I know I want to be a professional photographer, but I don't really know what direction I want to take that. Studio, weddings, more landscapes, book covers, high fashion."

He shrugged and looked back at her, his dark brown eyes boring a hole in her. "Wouldn't art school help you figure that out?"

"It might, or it might confuse the issue even more. So far, I've mostly done nature. Landscapes, flowers, stuff like that and they've sold. I've taken some old buildings; barns, churches, houses. People seem to like those, too. Birthday parties and weddings for people in our town of course, the kind of thing anyone with a decent eye and camera get sucked into. Whether they like it or not."

"Did you like it?"

She sighed. "I didn't hate it, but no, I can't imagine doing weddings and birthday parties all the time. I'm a more solitary person than that. Taking pictures of Alyssa doing rodeo was fun, but partly because she is my best friend."

"Speaking of rodeo, that stunt yesterday—"

"Yes, yes, I know, foolish of me. Didn't know the horse well enough. Even though I'd been riding her for an hour and Alyssa said both the mares we were riding had participated in rodeo, when Emma had done some trick riding. And we'd already played around with them some to see how they handled. We thought Tony would enjoy it and we're talking about entering the rodeo competition at the harvest festival, if I'm still here." She gave him an imperious glare. "We are not quite as stupid as you might think, Adam."

"Well I'm glad to hear that, but think about what it might have looked like to me not knowing your skill or training or how the horses might react."

"Fine, I can see your point, but maybe you should realize that twenty-two-year-old women are not babies and are capable of knowing their own limits. Do you treat your sister like she's too young to know what she's doing?"

"Well, no, but I know what she's capable of." He ran his fingers through his hair and slapped his hat on his leg before putting it back on his head. "I need to get moving, good luck with your decisions."

She wanted to tell him good luck on minding his own business but decided that was a little too obnoxious, since he was mostly being pleasant for a change. He walked a few steps from her then turned around and gave her a half smile that did something to her insides she didn't plan to think about.

"There is plenty of nature and lots of old buildings around for you to photograph while you're here for the next few months. Alyssa shouldn't be able to keep you busy every minute with wedding plans and picture taking. Feel free to ask any of us for suggestions or directions."

"Thanks, I'll do that." As he walked away she admired his well put together self, he had a nice butt for starters and an easy gait that got a woman to wondering about things. He'd even been decent to her, which tended to make her notice his attractiveness even more. Not that she would be interested in anyone normally so grumpy and judgmental.

ADAM CONTINUED on to his truck, the woman had just put him in his place about several issues. She might have a point, but he was still the oldest brother and he took his responsibilities, as such, seriously. He didn't need a lawsuit from her breaking her neck on his ranch. He didn't need his brother to be married to the wrong woman. He didn't need to find Rachel such an attractive woman, even though she was one. He didn't need any more complications in life. What he did need was to find a way to be at peace with Beau's decision and be a good best man for his brother. Beau was hell bent on marrying Alyssa and that was that, so maybe it was time to stop grousing about her and get on board. Everyone else in the family thought it was great so maybe he *was* wrong. He sure as hell hoped he was.

He got in his truck and headed down the drive, he was meeting some of the local cattle ranchers for breakfast in Granby. They tried to meet after calving season each year to have a powwow about how things had gone. It was only about a twenty-minute drive and he was going to do his best not to think about how attractive Rachel had looked out in the early morning sunshine. Nope, he didn't want to think about her lovely legs and fine ass as she bent over to look into the viewfinder of her camera. He didn't want to think about her thick brown hair that had red highlights where the sun burnished it. And he didn't want to think about her large hazel eyes, and that sweetheart mouth. Or that he wanted to ravish her just to shut her up, well maybe that wasn't the *only* reason, but it was a good one. Nope, he wasn't going to think about those things. Not even her obvious intelligence, clear thinking and dedication to her art.

He hit his hand on the steering wheel. *Focus on something else...* but what? Maybe that damn drone. He should ask the rest of the ranchers at breakfast this morning to find out if any of them had seen it on their property. Or if they had any idea why it might be on his. This was the second time it had been seen on their land, the first time it had been flying low and had startled the cattle, this time it was his horse. Neither time had it caused a serious problem, but it could have, if things had gone a little differently. He'd checked on his horse after the call and he was fine. The hand that had rubbed him down had said he'd been skittish at first, but had calmed down once he'd been groomed and put in his stall.

He'd decided the first time had been a fluke, but he couldn't say that now with the second time. What was it doing? He hadn't gotten a good look at it since he'd been trying to avoid it being embedded in his forehead or Jake's. It just didn't add up; the first time it had been in the pasture and this time it had been in the trees next to the river.

Maybe it was someone in the National Forest whose drone had gotten away from them. They did border that land, but the river was pretty far away. He just didn't get it.

RACHEL KNEW it was time to pack up her equipment, so she could meet Beau and Alyssa to take the engagement photos. She swapped out her telephoto lens for the regular one and gathered up everything else. She and Alyssa had talked about a lot of different ideas, from formal shots to super casual. They were going to take lots, so there would be plenty to choose from. Some were going to be in front of the family room fireplace, some outside, there were plenty of beautiful places on the ranch. Rachel had even rigged up a black screen and had some other colors to switch it out, including a green screen. She had her light boxes in the family room.

Alyssa and Beau were waiting for her in the family room, all dressed up in their fancy clothes. "Well, don't you two clean up well?"

Beau grumped, "Don't get used to it. I did it, but I don't think these clothes are going to be the ones we want for engagement photos, they aren't natural looking for either one of us. Although Alyssa does look beautiful. But she won't give me even one little kiss, I might mess up her makeup. What kind of a veterinarian wears makeup anyway?"

Alyssa elbowed him. "One that is getting her engagement pictures taken. Now hush up and let's do these formal ones so we can put on some real clothes."

Rachel laughed, Alyssa had never been real big on formal attire. They took every pose they could think of. Then changed into slightly less fancy clothes and did it all again. They went through several more rotations of clothing changes, finishing with their jeans and boots.

"Okay, for the outdoor shots we need to narrow down the clothing changes, what did you guys like the best?" Rachel asked.

Beau said, "I like that black print dress with your cowboy boots. Can we take some outdoor pictures with that one?"

Alyssa nodded. "I like it too, it's kind of girly but with my boots on it makes it more me. To tell the truth I like you in your old jeans and sleeveless shirt."

"I think that combination might make a very interesting photo. Let's try it, Beau bring along your nicer jeans and a couple of shirts. Alyssa bring your jeans outfit. And that white shirt you have and your cutoffs. Both of you bring your hats. It's who you are."

They did as they were told. They took pictures in the field where they were growing hay, with the mountains in the background, then some by the fence. The day was slightly cloudy but that was actually better than too much sun.

They swapped out their outfits and took some on the dirt road, holding hands and playing around. But nothing seemed quite right.

Alyssa said, "Let's take some by the river. It's so pretty down there." They brought all their crap and got in Alyssa's SUV for the drive to the river. They took lots of pictures by the river in several outfits and then walked out of the trees to find Beau's pet cow, Dolly, by the Equinox. He'd rescued Dolly when she was just a calf and though they had bred her, she was far more pet than any other heifer on the ranch.

Alyssa grinned. "Oh, let's take some pictures with Dolly. Not for the engagement photo, but I want to put one on Facebook."

As Rachel snapped the pictures with Dolly and the couple, she just knew Alyssa would pick one of these. Now that they were just playing around with the cow they had relaxed, and their interaction with Beau's large pet was adorable. She hadn't done a lot of engagement pictures and realized if she was going to do more she would need to find a way to get the couple to relax and just have fun together. The ones on the road were better because they did play around some, but these were the best. Dolly was going to be a star.

CHAPTER 4

Adam drove into the yard just as Alyssa, Beau, and Rachel pulled up in Alyssa's Equinox. Beau had an armful of clothes when he stepped out of the SUV.

"Hey, Adam, how did the breakfast meeting go?" Beau asked.

"It went well." He walked over to the SUV and took some of the photography equipment from Rachel. "Let me give you a hand. Did you get some good shots?"

Beau groaned. "Good lord, I hope so. I've never had so many pictures taken of me in my life. My face is aching from smiling, and I'm so tired of changing clothes, I may sleep in these tonight."

Rachel rolled her eyes at Beau, then turned to him to answer his question. "I think I've got something that will work. You're welcome to join us in the viewing. They are raw, but the plan is to pick out the best ones for me to process."

"Well I'm not a great judge—"

Beau interrupted. "That's a great idea, it would help to have a second male opinion. And someone who wasn't part of the shoot. While she sets it up you can fill me in on the breakfast and whatever else you've been doing, while I've been changing clothes and smiling."

"I suppose I can do that. I'm caught up with everything for a while and I've no planned calls scheduled for today." Adam relented, he thought he caught a note of desperation in Beau's tone. He wasn't sure he wanted to look at all those pictures, but maybe that's why Beau wanted him to join them, to have someone to commiserate with. He didn't plan to give his opinion though, he didn't want to offend Rachel if they were mediocre.

While Rachel set up the pictures to display on the big screen TV, Adam filled Beau in on the rancher's meeting he'd gone to. How everyone's calving season had gone. When they were planning to ship the cattle to market. The illegal beaver trapping update and other cattle ranch issues.

After he was finished with all the news Adam said, "I asked them if they'd seen that darn drone, but no one else has seen anything. They all said they would keep their eyes open and let us know if they encountered it."

Beau shook his head. "I really thought one of the other ranches would have run into it. What do you think it means that it's just us?"

"I have no idea. We don't have any enemies that I'm aware of anyway. We've got nothing so special someone would need to be spying. Maybe it's just kids, or someone who can't control their drone, over in the National Forrest or in one of the houses on the main road."

"You don't think Nate would be behind it, do you?" Beau asked, referring to the man who had been harassing their sister for the last four years. She'd finally just told them about it a few weeks ago.

"No, the first time Lloyd and Kent spotted it was before Alyssa and Emma went to town and Emma got the restraining order. So, it really doesn't make sense. I don't think Nate's got the cash to buy one or the patience to fly one."

Beau nodded. "Yeah, you're probably right, plus it's never been around her, always out in the pasture."

"Exactly, if it was directed at Emma it would be around the house," Adam said. "We'll just have to keep our eyes open and see if we can figure out what it's doing."

Rachel said, "Show time."

Alyssa clapped her hands. "I'm so excited."

Beau grimaced. "I hate looking at pictures of me."

Adam laughed and punched his brother in the arm. "Then just look at Alyssa."

"That would make it better, but not doing it at all would be best."

"Man up, brother. It's all part of the process." They took a seat on the couch as Rachel brought up the formal pictures they'd taken in the house.

Rachel fidgeted, was she nervous? He supposed that might be a normal reaction for her to have to show off her work. But she needn't worry, they weren't art critics and they were prepared to be supportive, at least he was. "Now don't forget these are raw, they'll look better after I process them. We are just looking to pick out the best. Let's think about picking at least one with each setting."

Adam was surprised at the quality of the photos, they looked totally professional. He honestly did not see what she needed to process. But Beau and Alyssa looked a little stiff, like they were being tortured. Still, some of them were nice. Some of them were so similar he didn't see the difference. But Alyssa and Rachel seemed to, as they went through each one. At first, they tried to get input from Beau and himself, but after the girls realized they weren't going to say much they whizzed through the pictures, with a definitive no or maybe. Once they got the first scene down to a few maybes they put them up side by side and selected the best ones.

He and Beau did manage to weigh in on the final selections for each setting, at least a little. Sometimes the girls agreed with them and sometimes they did not. After one time the girls completely ignored their opinion Adam looked at Beau who shrugged. Adam was actually relieved that they weren't that much of the process, since all that mattered was that Alyssa was happy.

They went through scene after scene and Adam could understand why Beau had been complaining about changing clothes so much, he wasn't sure he wouldn't have killed someone if it had been him getting the pictures taken. These girls were thorough. Still he just didn't see anything that really stood out for him, he supposed any of them would do.

When they finished with the pictures that had been taken by the river Beau sighed. "That's it then."

Rachel shook her head. "There's one more set."

Alyssa frowned. "No there isn't, the river was the last—"

Rachel clicked into the pictures with Dolly. Alyssa smiled. "Oh Dolly, but we weren't going to use..."

Rachel clicked through a few more pictures of the two of them mugging with the cow.

Alyssa grinned. "They're the best of the whole bunch."

Rachel beamed. "Yes, they are, you two finally relaxed and you look so joyful posing with Dolly."

Adam had to admit she was right. They looked so at ease and happy in the pictures with Dolly. Rachel clicked forward again.

"Aww, look at that one." Alyssa sighed.

Adam was certain they had found the winner. Beau was on one side of Dolly with Alyssa on the other and they had leaned over the cow for a kiss. Dolly looked like she had a smile on her face.

Beau laughed. "She looks rather proud of herself, doesn't she? Dolly, the matchmaking heifer."

Alyssa laughed too, but hers was a little watery sounding. "I think that's the one."

Rachel nodded. "That's what I thought, too."

Alyssa folded her arms. "Then why didn't you start with that one?"

"Because you'll want some of the others as well and I wanted you to look at them all without bias."

Adam smiled inwardly. The woman was pretty clever, if she'd started at the end no one would have wanted to sit through all the others to select the best one. And she was right they would want some of the ones without the bovine for various things, like the newspaper announcement for one.

Alyssa huffed. "I suppose you're right."

"Of course, I am, I know you, Alyssa."

Adam found the exchange between the women highly interesting as well as amusing. Rachel didn't back down, but she was subtle about it. The next few months with both of them in the house might be highly entertaining.

RACHEL WAS happy with the decisions they'd made. She'd been surprised by Adam's attitude, he'd been very complimentary about the pictures she'd taken. He'd also been nice to Alyssa and Beau about the wedding. Maybe, just maybe, he was getting over himself and his judgmental attitude.

She cleaned up her stuff from the viewing area and then took down the screens she'd used. She definitely wanted to process one of the pictures with the green screen in case they wanted to put it on something without having to pull their images out of a picture. It was so much easier with the green screen. She folded up her light boxes and put them in their carrying cases. It was going to take her a few trips to her room to get it all in there. But she didn't mind, it was all part of the job and she was feeling exhilarated from the success of the shoot. Some day—when she had some extra money—she should probably purchase some kind of cart or collapsible hand truck. She didn't use all her equipment on the same day too often, so it wasn't much of a priority, but today it would have been handy.

She finished packing up the last of her things and started gathering up her first load when Adam pulled a little flat bed hand truck into the room. "Good you're still here. I had to clean this up a bit to bring into the house, but I thought you could use it while you're here and need to drag around a bunch of equipment."

Rachel just stared at the man. He was being nice, and it was starting to freak her out a little. He shifted from foot to foot and his shoulders looked tense, she realized she hadn't answered him. "Thanks, that's very thoughtful of you. I was kind of dreading hauling all this to my room."

His shoulders relaxed, and he smiled. That smile was a killer, out in the yard had been bad enough, but up close and personal it was just plain deadly. Lust shot through her and pooled in her belly. She fumbled with the cases she was holding and tried to keep him from noticing her reaction to his smile. Piling her equipment on the platform gave her an excuse not to look at him and if she got it all loaded quickly she could get away from him to take it all to her room. She needed to put some space between them—with a quickness—before she did something foolish. After all, he had some weird hang-up about age and he was two years older than Beau, that made them nine years apart. He would certainly think she was an idiot if she acted on her impulses.

Once she got it all loaded she half turned towards him

and said breezily, "Thanks for the loan of the hand truck, it will come in very handy." Then she practically bolted from the room.

She heard him say, "You're welcome." But she didn't turn back to look at him, she needed distance from the hot man with the killer smile, who had started being nice for some strange reason. It was much easier to ignore his good looks when he was being a jerk.

CHAPTER 5

Rachel had the next day all to herself. She took some landscapes in the morning—when the light was the best—then planned to spend all afternoon working on processing the pictures she had taken the day before. Alyssa was working on the final report for her internship that had to be turned in this week. Beau also had to write up his experience and evaluation of her as an intern. So, everyone was busy working on their computers. Her new desk was supposed to arrive today, she thought, and it couldn't come too soon. The little writing desk was just too cramped. She still loved it, but not as a work surface. She needed more space. Adam had been right about it not really working for her—not that she wanted to admit that—but it didn't make it less true.

After working on the photos for about four hours—on the tiny desk—she needed a break. She grabbed her camera bag and set out to find a distraction. Hopefully she would have the new desk to work on tomorrow.

She heard Tony laugh and decided to follow that sound. He was in the kitchen where he and Meg were making chocolate chip cookies. He stood on a chair next to the island counter and he was covered in flour. Meg had a fair amount on her too, and Rachel wondered what had happened.

"Mind if I watch?" she asked, as she took her camera out of the bag and adjusted it to take indoor pictures with no flash. It was bright in the kitchen with sunlight coming in the windows, so she would get some images, probably not as good as she would have gotten with the flash, but Tony might be distracted by the light and she didn't want to cause another flour explosion.

Meg smiled. "Sure. We're making cookies."

"It looks like a flour tornado went through."

Meg barked out a laugh and nodded. "Yes, one did."

Tony yelled, "It was me. I was the toe-nado. Flour got everywhere." His gleeful expression changed. "Mama is not going to be happy." He shook his head sadly.

"We'll get it all cleaned up before your mother comes home. Don't you worry." Meg patted his arm.

"Okay, Nana. Is it time to put in the chocolate chips?"

Meg smiled at the little boy. "Almost time, just a little more stirring first."

Rachel took some pictures of the process and the mess. Tony's eyes lit up when it was time to pour in the chocolate chips. Once the bag was open he took out a small handful and put them in his mouth, then poured the rest into the dough.

He chewed up his candy and then grinned at Rachel with a chocolaty smile. "The cookie maker always has to eat a few chips. To make sure they are good for the cookies."

"Do they now?" she said as she snapped a few pictures of the boy.

He nodded and then said dramatically, "But now we have to wait forever while the cookies bake."

Meg laughed. "Nine minutes is not forever, Tony."

"I know, Nana. But it seems like forever."

Rachel had to agree with that. Waiting for cookies to bake and be cool enough to eat, did seem like forever sometimes.

"Did you take my picture, Rachel?" He asked.

"Yes, do you mind?"

"No, but you can't show mama, 'cause she'll see the toe-nado mess." Tony drew pictures with his finger in the flour coating the counter.

"Don't you ever make cookies with your mama?" she asked.

"Yes, but mama doesn't let me help as much. I just do the chocolate with her. Not the flour." He hopped down from his chair and raced around the room.

Rachel looked at the kitchen disaster then back at Meg. As Tony ran around and around the kitchen island, flour flew off of him leaving the air murky. Rachel decided Emma was the wiser of the two. Then again, she knew grand-mothers always let their grandchildren get away with more than their children ever did. And she figured that is exactly how it should be.

ADAM STOPPED dead in his tracks when he found Rachel, Tony, and his mother eating chocolate chip cookies in a room that appeared to have had a flour bomb go off in it. Tony was nearly covered from head to toe except for the chocolate all over his mouth and hands. His mom had some on her clothes and in her hair. Rachel only had a little on one knee and an elbow, apparently, she'd come in after the explosion.

He walked into the room. "So, I smelled chocolate chip cookies clear out in the barn, and thought I better come investigate. Tony, did you help Nana make cookies?'

"I did. I helped with the flour and the chocolate," his nephew crowed.

Adam enjoyed the little boy's pride in helping his grandmother. "I never would have guessed. Do I get to taste one?"

Tony nodded excitedly. "Yes, uncle A, you can have one."

Rachel looked at him and raised an eyebrow. "Uncle A?"

He shrugged. "I'm uncle A, Beau is uncle B and Drew is uncle D. For Cade and Chase, he has to use their names, two uncle C's wouldn't work."

"I guess uncle C1 and C2 would be kind of weird and they might fight over who was one and who was two." Rachel laughed, and the sound slid through Adam making goosebumps break out on his whole body.

He gritted his teeth and nodded. He didn't want to have that kind of reaction to this woman. She was too young for the likes of him. Hell, he thought Alyssa was too young for Beau. The girls were the same age and he was two years older than his brother. That was just wrong. He frowned and ordered his body to get under control, took a cookie and ate it, to give him a minute to collect himself.

When he was finished he turned and spoke sharply to Rachel. "I came in because the delivery people called to say they would be here in fifteen minutes with your new desk. Do you know where you want it or need to move anything?"

Rachel raised an eyebrow at him, probably wondering about his change in attitude. Well she would just have to wonder, he was going to start treating her like a child to remind himself to keep back.

"I have the space cleared, so it can be delivered with no problems."

"Good. If you all can stay here in the kitchen, I'll have them bring it in through the front door." Rachel started to stand. "You too, Rachel. Unless you think I can't tell where the desk should go."

"No, it's obvious. I just thought—"

He cut her off. "I've got it. The less people underfoot the better."

She flinched and folded her arms. "Fine."

Now he'd pissed her off, any time a woman said "fine" in that tone of voice it was anything but. He decided that was a good thing though. If she was ticked at him maybe she wouldn't go around laughing all the time.

~

RACHEL WATCHED the man walk out of the room. *Did he really say I would get underfoot? Like I'm five, and don't know how to get out of the way?* She honestly could not believe he'd said that. *Underfoot? Really?*

"I must admit that was weird," Meg said turning her gaze back to Rachel. Rachel realized she must have spoken out loud.

She was just so shocked. He'd seemed pleasant enough when he walked in, but then he'd gotten nasty again. She supposed he'd used up his allotted quota of niceness yesterday.

Meg shook her head. "I know I'm his mother and I *should* be on his side, but I don't think I would let him get away with treating me that way. If I was you."

Rachel turned her head slowly to Meg, weighing her options and Meg's opinion. "You know, I think you're right. It's my room, and I have a vested interest in the delivery, not Mr. Imperious."

Meg grinned. "Sometimes Adam can get a little full of himself, as do most men. I think you're just the one to take him down a peg or two."

"I can do that." She brushed the flour off her clothes, as

she walked out of the kitchen with her camera bag. *A little full of himself, indeed.*

She sauntered into her room where Adam was standing. "I decided that the delivery men would want to know how *I* want *my* desk positioned in *my* room, so if you think two people are going to get underfoot, you need to be the one to leave."

He sighed. "I should have known you wouldn't take that comment lying down."

"I am not a five-year-old that gets underfoot, Adam. I'm an adult woman who can determine how to ride a horse and what I am capable of. I can direct workmen without getting in the way. And I am a competent photographer. So, I expect you to treat me with respect and not like a child."

"Got it." The doorbell chimed. "I'll go let the delivery men in."

"Thank you."

When he'd left the room, she wondered if her little speech would help or if she'd wasted her breath. She felt better about not letting him put her down or treat her badly, so she decided it was worth it even if he was determined to be a jerk.

The delivery men brought the desk into her room and she was shocked. It was huge. On both sides of where the chair went were pedestals, one side had a bunch of shallow drawers, the other side had a filing cabinet drawer on the bottom and a shelf above that. This was a desk for a serious professional. She was so shocked at Adam's generosity, she could hardly direct the men. There was also a very nice rolling desk chair in a box and a pad to go under it, so it would roll smoothly on the carpet.

When the men were finished setting the desk up, Adam said, "I'll walk them out and bring up some tools to put the chair together."

She nodded. "Okay." She was so flabbergasted it came out as almost a whisper.

He arched a brow at her and left with the men. She went over to the desk and ran her hands over it, then she opened the drawers and filing cabinet. It was an amazing piece of furniture, much nicer than what she had at home, and Adam had bought it without her even asking.

She honestly didn't know how to feel, she was so confused.

~

ADAM LET THE MEN OUT, grabbed up the tool box, and went back to Rachel's room. She'd acted very odd when the men had brought the desk in. He didn't know if she liked it or hated it. He thought it was a nice desk and it had lots of drawers and a filing cabinet, and everything he thought she would need to stay a few months and work on her photography.

He walked into her room and she didn't even acknowledge him, she just stood there like a zombie running one hand over the top of the desk.

He cleared his throat, so he didn't startle her and asked, "So will it work?"

She turned her head and just looked at him.

"Rachel? What's wrong?"

She shook her head. "I just don't understand you. One minute you're nice, the next you're treating me like a pest. When I got here three days ago you were crabby and short with me. But while I was unloading my car you were ordering me a thousand-dollar desk and having the family put all my things away in an orderly fashion. Downstairs a few minutes ago you were friendly and laughing one minute, and calling me a child the next. Frankly, you're giving me whiplash."

Oh, hell, how was he going to explain? He knew he was acting irrationally, but he didn't want to tell her he found her attractive and was fighting that with everything he had. Could he just avoid the whole thing with deflection? He was damn sure going to try.

"I'm not sure what to say. Other than, will the desk work?"

She frowned at him, then turned toward the desk. "It's perfect."

"Good. This room needed a decent desk. Until you came with all your equipment we just never noticed." He hoped she would leave it at that, and turned to the chair to start putting it together. Hopefully it would be as quickly assembled as the advertisement had said.

CHAPTER 6

Rachel spent the next few days exploring the ranch in the morning—camera in hand—and the afternoon happily working at her new desk. She processed the pictures for Alyssa and Beau then emailed them the files, so they could see them on a full screen or even take them to the flat screen TV for extra-large viewing. Then she spent the rest of her time playing with the pictures she'd been taking in her morning adventures. She wanted to send some of them off to be printed and shipped to the art gallery in her home town of Chedwick, Washington. They were always happy to have new inventory to sell.

The only thing she wished for, was her desktop machine and dual monitors. It had more horse power than her laptop. Even though her laptop was high end, it had a small screen. What she wouldn't give for her extra monitors. And maybe her printer, she liked to print some images, so she could play around with them and see the differences in a printed copy. Not that her printer would do the photos justice or be sale ready, but for her purposes it was great.

Alyssa came bounding into her room one day. "It's done and emailed to the school. Yay, I feel like I've been let out of jail. You would not believe how long and detailed of a report they wanted. I thought I would never get it done."

Rachel rolled her eyes. "It was a report for a whole semester's work. I would hope it was detailed. Did Beau get his sent in, too?"

"Yes, two days ago. His wasn't quite as long as mine. But he let me read it and it was glowing. You would think I walked on water. I did work hard while I was here, so he said it was deserved. But I rewarded him very well, anyway." She grinned naughtily.

Rachel chuckled. "Well of course you did, and I imagine he rewarded you right back."

Alyssa sighed dreamily. "Yes, he did. But I'm not going to kiss and tell."

Rachel huffed. "Since when? Where is the fun in that?"

"Since, I'm marrying the man and you are here in the house with us both. It seems a little awkward to say too much."

"That's probably true. I might have to critique him or stand in awe."

Alyssa gave her a very naughty look. "Stand in awe for sure. And you might get jealous."

Rachel barked out a laugh. "Good to know you are a very satisfied woman."

"I am indeed. Now let's get out of here for a while. I feel like I've been cooped up for days and days."

"Sounds good, what do you want to do? Take the horses out? Go into town and buy candy? You need to show me this candy buffet you keep talking about. But then we'd have to take everyone's order and that might take all night."

Alyssa nodded. "True enough. Let's take the horses out, and we can go into town tomorrow. You should see it, it's such a cute little town. Should we invite Emma and Tony and make it an event?"

"Yes, that would be fun, and Emma can collect the candy orders again."

"I like the way you think."

"That's why we've been friends since kindergarten," Rachel said wisely and then grinned. Alyssa grinned right back at her.

~

ADAM FINISHED up the accounting books for the week and decided he had time to take his horse out for a run. Being the business manager for the ranch took so much time, it seemed like he was always indoors. But he had everything caught up, finally.

He got a text from his sister.

Emma: Girl's day in town tomorrow escorted by Tony. Taking candy orders.

Adam laughed. She'd be getting a flurry of texts while everyone ordered. They all knew to text her directly, so everyone wouldn't be bombarded with candy text messages. He sent her his request and walked out to the barn to get his horse.

He stopped short when he heard women's voices in the barn. It sounded like Alyssa and Rachel. Was it too late to beat a hasty retreat? Yes, apparently it was. Rachel walked out of the stall leading the same chestnut mare she'd ridden the other day, with Alyssa right behind her. He tipped his hat to them as they walked by on their way out to the pasture. "Afternoon, ladies."

Alyssa chirped, "Hi Adam. I finally got my paper done so we're taking the horses out."

Adam nodded. “I finally got the books up to date, so I’m doing the same thing.”

“You’re welcome to join us,” Alyssa said.

It was a nice offer, but he just wanted to take a ride, not chat, not play tour guide. Just get on his horse and ride. Would they be offended if he said no, or relieved?

Rachel rolled her eyes at him. “Don’t strain anything Adam. It was a simple question. From your soon to be sister-in-law who comes from a family of six siblings and she’s a middle, so she’s always wanting to make everyone feel welcome. I, on the other hand, am a single child. So, I don’t have that inclination, and I don’t give a rat’s ass whether you come or not.”

Adam raised an eyebrow at her and decided to lie to her face, she needed to learn some manners, the sassy little miss. “I was just debating if Alyssa was simply being nice, or if you both wanted me to come along. I guess your comment seals it. Have a nice ride, ladies.”

He saw Alyssa glare at Rachel, who sighed. “No, please do come along, apparently Alyssa would like you to join us and it’s okay with me.”

Well damn, now he was stuck, that’d teach him for lying. “How could I pass up such a gracious invitation?”

He went into the barn, saddled his horse, and led him to where the girls were patiently waiting. Lucky him.

They started out across the pasture and gave the horses their heads, at least enough that they could get some exercise, and not scare the cattle. They were at a nice steady canter, when suddenly Alyssa dropped back. He looked back to see what was going on and saw her turn toward the left, heading for some cattle. He slowed to follow and noticed Rachel was doing the same.

He saw Alyssa leap off her horse with the medical saddle

bag in her hand. When he and Rachel got in close she called out to them. "Adam, call Beau to bring the truck. Rachel, I need you to give me a hand."

Adam didn't question her, he called his brother and gave him the coordinates of where they were. He didn't know what was wrong just that Alyssa said to get him there with the truck. He gathered up the reins for the three horses and tied them to a tree. Then he hurried over to see what the problem was. One of the one-year-olds was bleeding heavily. Alyssa had already washed out the wound and started stitching, by the time he got there. The bleeding had stopped. Rachel was helping to hold the wound closed so Alyssa could close up the cut. Beau arrived with the truck just as she finished stitching.

Alyssa said, "We need to get him back to the barn. He lost a lot of blood."

Beau nodded and the four of them got the animal into the truck.

Alyssa climbed in the back. She looked back at him and nodded toward Rachel. "She's squeamish around blood, take care of her."

He looked over at Rachel, and sure enough, her face was white as a sheet, and she was staring at her hands.

"Got it," he said, as the truck pulled away.

He went over to Rachel and drew her over toward the horses where he knew there was some water. She walked woodenly beside him, he just hoped she wouldn't pass out. He grabbed the canteen and then pushed her down on some grass. He poured water over her hands and used his handkerchief to wipe the blood and water off her. When he had all the blood removed, he tried to get her to talk to him, but she just kept staring at her now clean hands.

"Rachel, snap out of it." She didn't respond, and he didn't

know what to do. He had to get her attention. He took her hands and they were like ice, so he rubbed them to get the circulation flowing again. She shivered so he dragged his jacket off and put it around her shoulders. He took her chin in his hand and pulled it up, so she was looking at him instead of her hands. Her eyes were blank.

"Rachel, come on, you need to come back. There's no more blood. Come on, sweetheart. Look at me."

That seemed to get her attention. Her eyes started to focus. "I'm cold."

He wrapped his arms around her to share his body heat. She fit very nicely in his arms, but he didn't want to think about that, or why he'd called her sweetheart. He could always tell himself it was to surprise her out of being in shock.

He started talking, just to give her something else to focus on and think about. She'd mentioned she wanted to explore the area, so he started talking about all the things he could think of that she might want to photograph. Gradually he could feel her warming up and focusing more on what he was saying. When she finally asked him a question, he knew she was back in control. So, he drew back from her enough that he could look at her face, and was thankful to see her skin had color and her eyes showed him she was interested in what he was saying.

He was so relieved she was recovering he wanted to kiss her. Not because he really wanted to kiss her, of course, but because he was so happy that she was fine. He looked at her mouth and saw her catch her breath. Oh no, this was not a good idea.

He pulled back further. "So, are you ready to take the horses back to the barn and see how that steer is doing?"

She blanched at his question. What a stupid thing for him

to say, to remind her of the blood. What a dumbass he was sometimes. But instead of freaking out she nodded and started to stand. Her legs seemed a little shaky, so he held onto her arms to steady her.

"I'm fine. I just don't like blood." Her tone dropped as she said, "At least I didn't pass out this time."

"You did great. You held it together when you were needed. That's what matters the most."

She laughed a little bitterly. "I guess."

"No seriously. It's a very valuable ability to put your personal reactions aside to help during a crisis."

She narrowed her eyes and looked at him. "Why are you being so nice? It makes me nervous."

He laughed and knew if she could mouth off that she was fine. Ignoring the question, he shook his head. "Let's get these horses back to the barn."

She went over to her horse to get on and apparently had just noticed his jacket over her shoulders. Rachel shrugged out of the garment and brought it over to him, she handed it to him then reached up and gave him a small peck on the lips. "Thanks for taking care of me."

As she walked back to her horse he tried to figure out what had just happened. That two-second touch of her lips had sent fire through his veins. It was the strangest thing he'd ever felt, and he wasn't sure he liked it. In fact, he was sure he didn't like it. He shook himself and untied the horses, secured Alyssa's horse to his saddle and swung on to his own. During the entire ride back to the house he told himself he did not like that kiss. Not one little bit. He still had not convinced himself, by the time they rode into the yard.

RACHEL COULDN'T FIGURE out what had possessed her to kiss Adam, even that little peck. She didn't like him. Most of the time he was a jerk. Yeah, he'd been nice to her. He'd washed the blood off her hands, and given her his jacket, and held her until she warmed up, and talked her out of it. But did she really have to go and kiss the man? He'd not said one word about it either. Did he think she was crazy? That she was coming on to him? Or that she was grateful? Which is what it had been, gratefulness, that's all, nothing more than that. And there had been no tingles at the mere touch of lips, no tingles whatsoever, just a remaining shiver from the blood touching shock. Yep, that's all it had been, not tingles. Not. Tingles.

She was not looking forward to grooming the horses next to the man. How could she even look him in the eye? What a mess she had created from her impulsive gratitude.

When they got to the yard he didn't quite look at her, but said over his shoulder. "You go on in the house and lay down, I'll take care of the horses."

"Oh, but…"

"No really, you've had a shock and shouldn't stress your body out anymore today. Go get something sweet to drink to bring up your blood sugar, and either lay down or sit, to let your body regulate. If I need help with the horses I'll get one the hired hands to help, or one of my worthless brothers."

This was a convenient way out of having to talk to him about the kiss and she was no fool. She was going to take it. "You're probably right. Thanks for everything."

"Thanks back, for helping Alyssa with the steer." That time he did look at her, probably to make sure he hadn't sent her over the edge again. She just waved her hand like, no big deal, slid off her horse, and wrapped her reins around the hitching rail next to the barn.

Beau and Alyssa were in the kitchen getting large glasses

of soda, probably for the very same reason Adam had told her to, only theirs was adrenaline not shock.

Rachel thoroughly washed her hands before Alyssa could hand her the glass. Once they were clean Alyssa shoved the drink into Rachel's hand and pushed her into a chair. "Are you all right?" Alyssa asked, looking intently into her eyes.

She took a big gulp of the sugary soda. "Yes mom, Adam talked me down. And then made me come in for a sweet drink and to relax. He's taking care of the horses."

Beau handed Alyssa a new glass of soda. "Good. I was worried."

"I didn't pass out or anything and Adam was nice to me." She nodded at Alyssa's glass. "Now have some of yours before your blood sugar bottoms out."

Alyssa laughed, flopped into a chair and took a large gulp. Beau set some cheese and crackers on the table, along with a large bowl of salsa, tortilla chips, and grapes. Then sat beside Alyssa and took her hand.

Rachel happily took some food and put it on the plate he had provided. She was feeling hungry. "So, what happened to that steer?"

Beau shook his head. "We don't know. It wasn't cat scratches. It might have been barbed wire, but the cut was too deep. The barbs on barbed wire are less than an inch long. From what Alyssa said it was deeper than that. I've sent some ranch hands, and Chase and Cade out to comb that area to see if they can find anything that might have caused it. We don't want more injured animals. Thanks for your help out there, Rachel. You did a good job and Alyssa says you're not a big fan of blood."

Rachel shook her head as she chewed on the cheese and cracker she'd just put in her mouth. Goodness, she was starving.

Beau said, "Well we appreciate your help. Another pair of hands in a situation like that can make a huge difference."

"You're welcome," Rachel replied.

Everyone was quiet as they ate the food on the table. Beau got up and refilled all the glasses and made a fourth one just as Adam walked into the room. After he'd washed his hands he drank down at least a quarter of the drink, before he asked the same questions Rachel had. Beau repeated the same answers while Adam shoveled in what food was left.

By the time Beau was finished speaking Adam was frowning. "I can't think of anything that would cause something like that cut. At least not anything natural."

Beau nodded. "I agree, let's hope someone finds something."

"Did you send out Thomas?" Adam asked.

Beau rolled his eyes. "Do I look stupid? Of course, I did. If anyone can track the blood to the cause, it will be him."

Adam nodded as he stuffed more food in his mouth.

Rachel looked at Beau for an explanation.

Alyssa said. "Thomas had a grandfather that taught him all about tracking. If something leaves a trail he can follow it. That steer probably left enough blood anyone would be able to track it, but with Thomas it will be certain."

"Good to know, and handy to have on board," Rachel said.

Beau nodded. "More than you could guess."

Rachel could feel her eyelids drooping and her body felt heavy. "I think I'll go to my room and rest for a bit." She thought her speech sounded a little slurred, but her brain felt fuzzy, so she couldn't tell for sure.

Alyssa got up. "I'm going, too."

Alyssa took hold of Rachel and dragged her to her room. "I'm okay, Alyssa."

"You will be after a short nap."

She nodded. "I am tired."

Alyssa smiled as she helped her out of her jeans and shirt, leaving Rachel in just her underwear. "Just a side effect from the shock. Nothing to worry about. I'll come wake you in an hour."

Rachel flopped down on the bed and Alyssa covered her with the blankets. She was asleep before she could hear Alyssa shut the door.

CHAPTER 7

The next day, Tony proudly escorted his three ladies into town. As they drove along he recited everything his mother had told him. "Mama said we can buy candy on our way home. That way we don't have to worry about it melting and getting yucky, when we show Rachel town. And have lunch. And play on the playground. We are gonna have lots of fun."

Alyssa who was sitting in the backseat with him said, "Yes we are. What is your favorite place to show Rachel today, Tony?"

"The candy!" he yelled and then clapped his hands in glee. Rachel grinned at the little boy's enthusiasm.

Alyssa laughed. "Yes of course, but after the candy and the park?"

"The lake is my favorite, Lyssa. After the park and candy store. Have you seen the lake, Lyssa?"

"No, I don't think I have, Tony. That sounds like fun, we'll have to go there."

"They have ice cream," he said slyly.

"In that case we'll have to go after lunch."

"Yeah, mama always says after lunch too. So, I don't ruin my ap-tite." He sounded so sad Rachel wanted to laugh out loud, but bit it back, so he wouldn't get confused.

"So what else should we show Rachel?"

He shrugged. "Dunno, just a bunch of stores."

Emma spoke up. "You haven't seen much of the town either, Alyssa. It's mostly all on one street, so I was thinking we can just start at the end. Go down one side then come back up the other. Once we've eaten and bought all the candy orders, we can load back into the car and drive around the back of Main Street, then down to the lake."

"Sounds like a plan." Alyssa said.

Rachel thought that sounded like a great suggestion, and since her camera and only one extra lens was in her purse, she wouldn't hold them up too much taking pictures. At least that's what she thought, until Emma turned the corner into town. Rachel's breath caught, and she couldn't look around fast enough. The town was picturesque. All the buildings sat along a board walk with old-fashioned hitching rails in front of them, gas-looking street lights, and large almost porches. Most of the stores had chairs out front where you could sit and watch the people walk by. Her fingers itched.

She asked, "Emma, can you let me out here? I want to take some pictures, then I'll walk down and join you."

Emma pulled off to the side. "Sure, we'll take Tony to the park, which is pretty close to the start of town. Get some of his energy out and we can start exploring when you join us."

"Perfect."

"Alyssa, do you want to go with us to the park or get out with Rachel?" Emma asked.

Alyssa answered quickly. "I'll go with you to the park. I know Rachel, and I would rather be somewhere with benches."

Everyone laughed as Rachel got out of the car and waved goodbye to them. "See you in a bit."

She slid her camera out of the bag, put the wide-angle lens on it and started snapping pictures. Some of the buildings had false fronts on them, almost like they were movie props. She was charmed. She didn't take nearly as many pictures as she wanted to, because she didn't want to keep everyone waiting for her. Some other day she could come back with more of her equipment and more time. She took just a couple shots of each thing that enchanted her, so she could plan out her future visit.

Walking toward the park she kept snapping pictures of interesting things, and even a few people. She couldn't use any of the peopled pictures in her work unless she got waivers from them, but she would enjoy looking at them

The park didn't have a lot of kids in it, she spotted Tony right away at the top of the climbing structure ready to slide down. She quickly zoomed in on him and held the button down to photograph the entire descent. There may be a couple of them Emma would like or even Travis and Meg.

When he hit the ground he yelled, "There she is!" And took off running toward her.

She put her camera in her bag, so she would have both hands free to catch him if she needed to. Which she did. He launched himself at her and she caught him and squeezed him tight. "Are you happy to see me?"

He grinned at her. "I am. We still have to explore. And get lunch. And candy. And ice cream. The park is fun, but that's a lot of stuff to do."

"It is indeed." She put him back on his feet and they walked hand in hand over to the bench where Alyssa and Emma had been sitting. "Tony is ready to go exploring."

"Great. Tony let me know if you get chilly and want your jacket," Emma said.

"Okay, mama. I'm kinda sweaty right now from some hard playing."

Emma nodded. "I'm sure you are."

"Oh, look Rachel, there's the candy store right across the street." Tony crowed pointing across the street to a large building that looked like it had living space above it. There were six or eight stairs up to the door level with three staircases, one on each end and one in the middle. It was the only building that had stairs, the rest had doors on the street level. Rachel wondered why it was built so different than all the others.

Rachel smiled down at the little boy. "Well, that makes it just perfect after we've explored we can buy all that candy for everyone on the ranch. Then walk across the street and get in the car to go drive down to the lake."

"And get ice cream," he yelled.

Emma admonished. "Tony, you need to start using your inside voice now, we are going to be going into the shops.

"Yes, mama," he said quietly. "Mama?"

"What, Tony?"

"Can we go into the place where the man makes the animals made of glass?" he asked.

Emma nodded. "I don't know why not."

"I think that would be great, does he make them while you watch?" Rachel asked as they stepped up onto the board walk.

Tony nodded happily, then looked very serious. "But you can't buy the ones he makes while we watch. They have to cool, but he always has some other cool ones. Sometimes he makes bowls or Christmas balls. It's kinda fun to watch."

The stores were all basically tourist shops with lots of Colorado souvenirs, from fool's gold to leather goods to plastic license plates with names on them. Interspersed between the tourist shops were candy stores with chocolates, or taffy, or Carmel corn. There was a quilt shop with yard goods, patterns and a work area, where classes were taught. There was a leather store where everything in the store was priced less than thirty dollars. Rachel found a camera bag that would be perfect for carrying a few items, when she didn't want to lug the big one with all the equipment.

There was an art gallery that had some very unique wooden art, and metal sculptures that were fascinating in their complexity. The art gallery had some photographs, but they weren't terribly unique, Rachel could probably sell her work in there if she wanted to.

At the end of one side of the street was a miniature golf course that was for sale. They looked through the fence surrounding it. Rachel was amazed at the delightful constructions within. Every hole seemed to have a Colorado theme, one was a Denver broncos helmet and goal posts and a football. The Colorado Rocky Mountains ran down the side of one hole. Another one was the state capital with its gold dome, a lot of the gold paint had worn away. Everything beyond the fence was in need of repair, but it had obviously been a very cute course to play on.

They spent about a half hour in the glass blower's shop, watching him make a robin. Tony was enthralled with the whole process and clapped his hands in glee when he realized the glass blower was making a bird. All three of them bought Tony a small animal, he was delighted.

Coming up the other side of the street were very similar shops. One was vacant, and Rachel asked what it had been.

Emma said, "I think it was a photography studio and art display."

"Really? That's awesome, did it have a portrait studio?"

"Yes, I think so, I seem to recall coming in to have our pictures taken. Mom would know the best. It might have had a dark room, I remember there being funny smells in there. It's been closed a while now."

"That's so cool I would love to have a dark room to experiment with film development, not that it's necessary these days, but it would still be fun to try it."

Alyssa grabbed Rachel's arm and started dragging her. "Come on, camera geek girl. I'm getting hungry, and there's a wonderful smell coming from this next building."

Emma laughed, and Rachel rolled her eyes. "Fine. I suppose I'm getting hungry too."

As they ate, Rachel kept thinking about the abandoned photo studio and how fun it would be to reopen it. Not that she was going to be staying in Colorado, but it was fun to think about. A lot of ideas popped into her head. Fortunately, no one noticed her distraction because Tony was entertaining the entire restaurant and its staff. He was telling the waitress all about the plan to stop by the candy store and then get ice cream by the lake, but first he had to eat all his lunch.

ADAM WAS PAYING bills and trying not to think about that kiss. It had only been a peck, not even a real kiss, so why couldn't he get it out of his mind. It was simply a small token of appreciation for taking care of her after a traumatic event. Not a real kiss, but something had lit inside him and he didn't know what to think or do. He was profoundly thankful that Rachel had spent the rest of the evening in her room last night, so he didn't have to hide his feelings from her. What those feelings meant, he had no idea, he wasn't even sure what they were. So how could he analyze them?

Pushing away from the desk he decided a ride would clear his mind, he wasn't going to get anything accomplished with his thoughts whirling around and around. He put a note on his computer that said, “Going for a ride be back in an hour.” with the time and then he walked through the house to the back door and pulled on his boots and a jacket. He was glad he didn’t encounter anyone in the house or the barn, he wasn’t in the mood for idle chatter.

Since he didn’t want to talk to anyone, he headed straight off their land and into the National Forest, it was less likely there would be anyone he would need to talk to in there. There was a trail he could take up to a small plateau that had a pretty view. The forest and mountains were on one side and their ranch on the other. He and his siblings had camped there often growing up, it was within sight of the ranch, but far enough away to feel adventurous.

They’d had quite the drunken party a few years ago. Drew’s best friend Zach had gone off to try his hand at being a rodeo star. He’d succeeded too, Zach was in the money more often than not these days. Adam could admit that he missed Zach, he’d been a good hand at the ranch, and a hard worker. He was sure his brother missed him even more, they’d done everything together. He hadn’t been back much since that night. Adam wasn’t sure why that was, he assumed it was just the demands of the sport, but he didn’t know that for certain. It seemed like he should be able to come home once in a while if he wanted to. Although Zach’s mother had moved away to live with his older sister, so maybe Zach just spent his off season there. Drew told them stories about Zach once in a while, so he knew he kept in touch with him.

When Adam reached the plateau, he saw there was someone camping up there. It was public ground so that was perfectly legal, but it seemed a little odd to him, there wasn’t much to do up there. No fishing, no facilities, not much of anything really. It was ideal for kids wanting to spend the night away from home, but a regular camp ground it was not.

Whoever it was that was camping was not anywhere to be seen. He dismounted and let his horse munch on the grasses up there. Adam turned his back on the tent and looked out over the land his family had owned for generations. He watched the cattle—down below—roam. There were some of the hands and probably some family in the hay fields, the crops were growing well. Some guys were probably riding the fences too looking for any breaches that needed repair. With the birthing season over they didn't need to work in shifts any longer, but there was still plenty of work to be done.

Speaking of work, he should probably get his butt back to his desk and finish paying the bills. Reluctantly he remounted his horse and started the ride back down the hill. He was feeling much more peaceful, so he should be able to do his job.

When he got back to the office cum library he shared with his parents there was a commotion going on. Both his parents were in the room with Thomas and Beau. They were all looking at the wall map of the ranch. It appeared Thomas had found the cause of the injury to the cow Alyssa had stitched up.

Adam walked up to the rear of the group and heard Thomas say, "It was a very odd place for something like that. I couldn't figure out why someone would leave that laying around."

Adam asked, "Sorry I missed the first part, what did you find and where?"

Thomas acknowledged Adam with a nod and said, "I found a sharpened pickax partially imbedded in the ground. It was in the trees by the river right about there." He pointed to a place on the map. "It was stuck pretty deep in the ground and took a bit of work to pull it out. I don't know what that one year old was doing in that area but there was a rock next to it making a small opening, so if that animal was determined to go through the gap the pickax would have easily carved into the skin."

Adam said, "That's not far from where I was when that drone startled Jake, and I ended up on foot."

Meg shook her head. "A drone and now a pickax, just what is going on around here?"

"I don't know sweetheart," Travis said. "But we'll get to the bottom of it, don't you worry."

Adam said, "Yes we will. Thomas, good job. Let the rest of the hands know what you found, tell them keep their eyes open, and report anything they find that seems odd. We're going to be busy with Alyssa's family coming soon and her graduation, so it will be up to you guys to be on the lookout."

Thomas nodded. "You've got it. I'll spread the word."

CHAPTER 8

Two days later, the Jeffersons' descended like a horde of locusts. They'd all driven in for Alyssa's graduation, which would take place in two days, and they had brought a whole load of her belongings with them. They'd driven three vehicles, all three extended cab pickups, with the truck beds full of Alyssa's things. One truck pulled a horse trailer with her horse in it.

Rachel laughed when Alyssa burst into tears seeing her family and her horse. She'd known the family was coming, but not her horse. Molly was getting on in years and Alyssa didn't see any real reason to have her brought halfway across the country. But she was so happy to see her.

The horse apparently felt the same way, because she started neighing before she was out of the trailer. When she finally backed out Alyssa threw her arms around the horse's neck and sobbed into her mane, while Rachel snapped pictures of the reunion.

When Alyssa had finally calmed down enough to ask why they'd taken the time and expense to bring her horse, her father ran his fingers through his hair and shook his head.

"It was the darndest thing, Alyssa. We packed up two trucks, thinking that was what we would need to get all your paraphernalia here. When all of a sudden Molly started having a fit. Neighing and kicking her stall door. We thought maybe something was wrong with her stall, so we brought her out, so someone could check it. She walked straight over to the horse trailer and butted her head against the door, then she looked back at us, neighed and did it again and again."

Her brother, Tim, laughed. "We finally figured out she wanted to come with us, so we loaded up my truck with food and water for the two-day journey and brought her along. Once she was in the horse trailer she settled right down. And there was nothing at all wrong with her stall. She just was determined not to be left behind."

Alyssa smiled through her tears. "Well, I did tell her I would only be gone four years."

Rachel kept snapping pictures as the two families were introduced to each other until Tim came over and pulled her hair.

She put down her camera and looked over at him. "What?"

"Hey brat, the gallery needs some more pics, asap. Summer is coming, and the town is already starting to fill up. And there are big holes on the walls where your stuff goes."

Not a surprise, she'd talked to the art gallery owners before she left and promised to send replacements. "I know. I've been working on some; the printer has an order that should arrive any day now."

"Yeah?" Tim's eyes lit up.

"Want to see?" She grinned at him.

"Of course, but maybe I should help unload Alyssa's crap first."

"I'll help too, and then we can go to my room to play show and tell."

He raised his eyebrows at her. "Sounds good to me and if you weren't my adopted little sister it would sound like you were inviting me for something else entirely."

She shuddered dramatically. "Eww, well, you don't have to worry about that."

"Exactly my thought, let's get this done, can't wait to see your etchings."

She smacked him in the stomach. "Knock it off, pseudo big brother."

He laughed like a loon which drew everyone's attention. He grinned. "Let's get this crap unloaded. I have a date with Rachel."

The Jeffersons' all laughed knowing the artists were going to closet themselves away to do their art thing. The Kiplings' looked confused.

Alyssa rolled her eyes. "Tim works in the art gallery where Rachel sells her work, they're going to do their creative thing."

Tim said, "Hey, I sell my work there, too."

The Jeffersons' all groaned at the same time. Hank said, "Just start carrying, artist. You can geek out in a minute."

Beau walked over to Adam, "Could you get the horse settled? While the rest of us carry in Alyssa's stuff?"

ADAM NODDED AT HIS BROTHER, glad he had something to do that didn't force him to interact with the rest of them. He didn't know why Tim Jefferson's crack about having a date with Rachel had pissed him off, but it had.

He went over to the mare. "So, you're Molly, are you?" The horse nodded like she understood. "Well I'm Adam, welcome to the Rockin' K. I'm going to find you a nice pleasant stall and give you some time to rest after that long journey. Sound good?" Again, the horse nodded, and Adam chuckled.

He led Molly into the barn and found her an empty stall with the rest of the horses. "So, Beau has an old cow named Dolly and Alyssa has you, an..." If she did understand he better not offend. "... a mature horse named Molly. Kinda starting to sound like a match made in heaven. Maybe I was wrong about the two of them." The horse nodded a third time and then bumped him with her nose.

He laughed. "Fine, I'll take that as a hint to back off and quit being grumpy about it." Molly nodded again and whinnied, and Adam decided she agreed with that idea.

He took the halter off and gave her a good brushing. Then he filled the water and food troughs and left the horse. Outside he found Alyssa's oldest brother Mike unloading the feed and straw from the pickup.

Adam joined him. "You sure you don't want to take this back? We can feed Alyssa's horse."

Mike shook his head. "Nope, we've got plenty and it's a pain to have it in the truck. By the time we drive over for graduation and get back to Washington it'll be almost two weeks since we loaded it, and that's too long out in the weather."

Adam looked at the clear blue sky. "Whatever you want."

Mike laughed. "I hear you never know about the weather up here in the high country of Colorado."

Adam nodded. "True, we do have unpredictable weather." He didn't want to say anything else, because he didn't know what all Alyssa had told her family about being caught alone in a late spring blizzard.

He was relieved when Mike started asking him questions about their ranch.

He spent a pleasant time talking with Mike about their respective ranches. The man was knowledgeable and had good insights. Adam took him around to show him their operations near the house, and they compared notes on how they ran things.

Adam said, "If you have time while you're here we can take some horses out and I can show you around."

"We aren't planning to intrude, we booked some rooms in town."

Adam jerked to a stop. "That's ridiculous. We've got the bunkhouse and four cabins on the property which are prepared for your family to stay in. Or you can all stay in the main house and us guys will take the bunkhouse. Didn't Alyssa tell you we planned to put you up?"

Mike shrugged. "I don't know. I just know we have rooms booked."

"Where?"

"The Singing River Ranch."

Adam pulled out his phone scrolled through his contacts and selected one.

"Singing River Ranch, how can I help you."

"Hi Karen, the Jeffersons' will be staying with us."

Karen said, "Sure thing, Adam. I thought it was odd when they booked, but I didn't know what to say, so I took the reservation. Your dad already called to cancel it."

Adam smirked at Mike. "Yeah, I don't know where they got that idea either. So, dad already called you?"

"Beau called too, right before you did."

He laughed and grinned at Mike. "And Beau. You might hear from Emma too, or the twins."

Karen said, "I don't have all day to spend my time talking to every Kipling in the family. I have work to do. Can you text the rest of them and let them know they don't all have to call?"

Darn it, he forgot this was a business transaction. He didn't want this to be a financial burden on her. "Sure thing. The cancellation isn't a problem, is it?"

"Nope, never figured you guys would let your soon-to-be in-laws off the ranch. I'm just glad they went there first rather than checking in here," she said.

He laughed. "You know us too well. Talk to ya later."

Adam disconnected, sent a text that said, "Karen's good" and looked at Mike. "Well, now that we have that little issue has been taken care of, do you want a bunk or a cabin?"

Mike shook his head. "I don't plan to choose. Your parents and mine probably have it all arranged by now."

And indeed, they had.

CHAPTER 9

The Jeffersons' were at the Rockin' K for two days before Alyssa's graduation. Adam enjoyed them a lot more than he thought he would. They could almost be the same family, they thought so much alike. Adam spent most of his time with Mike, Alyssa's oldest brother. They were very close in age and since they were both the oldest sibling of six they had a lot in common.

One afternoon Adam decided to be frank with Mike about his misgivings. "So how do you feel about your sister marrying a man seven years older than she is?"

Mike shrugged. "I didn't think much about it, Alyssa has always been more mature than her age. It actually would seem odd if she married someone younger, even Chase and Cade seem too young and immature for her. They are what, two or three years younger, than Beau?"

"Two, yes. It just seems like a big age gap. He was in high school when she was in second grade."

"Well if they had been dating back then, I would have been concerned, but they weren't. Alyssa was very precocious even at eight years old. Very sensitive and intuitive. She noticed our dad's attraction to Ellen, even before he did, I think. She said that Ellen and Dad looked at each other differently than they did anyone else. And she was right."

"She mentioned something like that her first night here." Maybe he was being over cautious, her brother and father didn't see anything wrong. And his dad and mom seemed to be happy about the situation. He apparently was the only one concerned. Maybe it was him, not them. He'd never had a serious relationship. He'd dated, but nothing was ever serious. He never allowed anyone to get too close and he had to wonder why that was. But not now, so he decided to change the subject. "What made her decide to become a veterinarian?"

Mike gave him a side glance. "She hasn't mentioned it?"

Adam shook his head. "Not that I know of. At least I've never heard anything about it. She did mention she had a story similar to Beau's. About saving Dolly, when she got clawed up by the big cat that killed her mother. But I've never heard it."

"Alyssa was an animal saver practically from the day she was born. Birds, bugs, even snakes." Mike shook his head. "When our mother died, she was six and pestered all of us about why the doctors couldn't save her. We figured she would become a doctor to find a cure. In fact, she and Rachel played with their Barbies like they were the doctors curing them of all kinds of problems. Those poor dolls had more broken legs and arms." He laughed and shook his head.

Mike continued, "But her bent stayed toward animals, and was solidified when a vet came out to the ranch for an animal that needed medical attention for several days. Since our town is so remote, he stayed at the ranch. She was about ten or maybe eleven, and she followed him around the entire time he was there, asking him question after question. The guy was great with her and answered all of them, he even let her help him as he treated the animal and looked over the rest of the herd. When he left, she talked about being a vet from that day forward and never changed her mind one bit."

Adam nodded. "Makes sense, she does seem very dedicated for being as young as she is."

Mike laughed. "Don't let her age fool you, she's been an adult, mentally, since she was eight years old."

~

RACHEL WAS happy to have Tim around for a few days. Alyssa was always supportive, but she didn't always get the artistic bent. Tim got it. They talked shop, they looked at her work and he gave her his opinion on some of her newest pictures. They went into town and he was as enamored with the old buildings and false fronts as she was.

She took him by the old photo studio that was for sale and talked in depth about what she would do with it if she had the means. And the desire to stay in Colorado. It was all pipe dreams and wild imaginings, she didn't plan to stay in Colorado. Her life and her family were in Washington.

"It's a great location in the middle of this street. I think it would draw foot traffic depending on what you offered," Tim said.

"I would love to display my art, but I was thinking it might also be fun to have one of those places that have costumes and sell tourists their pictures in the old-fashioned wild west clothes. Of course, that would be mostly a summer thing. But maybe the winter could be spent taking school pictures and family portraits for Christmas cards and the like. If it has a dark room I would love to play in one of those, just because no one takes film anymore and it's a dying art. That would be a hobby more than anything else. Although restoring old photographs might be fun to learn. Not just uploading them and then using a program to restore them and then print a new copy, lots of people do that and I wouldn't be averse to it. But what I would find fascinating would be actually taking the original and preserving it."

"You've got lots of ideas. Have you called the number to see what it really has and how much it would cost?"

"No, silly, I'm not staying here." If she knew more about it, she might want it even more than she already did. No, she didn't want to call.

He frowned. "Still a phone call can't hurt you and it would be fun to see what the building has and what the going price is."

"Yeah, but I don't want to get the real estate person all excited about a potential sale, when there isn't going to be one."

"Yeah, but."

She needed to get him off the subject before he had her calling the number. "Wait, let me show you something else that's for sale, Mr. Woodworker."

"Show away."

They walked down the street to the miniature golf course. He looked at her like she'd lost her mind, until they looked through the fence. When he saw all the wooden designs for each hole his attitude changed.

"Damn, would I like to get my hands on all that and restore it. I hate to see all that work going to ruin."

"Right?!? I just knew you would feel that way too. I'm not even a woodworker but my fingers still itch to fix it."

"Right there with you girlfriend, right there with you."

They looked through every break in the fence that surrounded the course and saw even more fun constructs, than she'd seen the first day. It looked like there were two courses, one that was everything Colorado and one that looked like it was based on the wild west.

Tim sighed. "That would certainly be a fun undertaking, but it's not really in my realm of expertise. Whittling figurines is not quite the same as restoring those large mechanical constructs."

"True." Rachel looked at the sad deserted golf course. "It's just pitiful to see it sitting there neglected."

"Yeah." Tim frowned. "You know Terry has all the tools to do something like that."

She laughed. "He does, too bad he's four states and two days away."

"I'm guessing they wouldn't transport too well either."

Her eyebrows shot up. "You mean like pulling them up and taking them with you? You aren't serious, are you? Aren't you kind of busy with working on the ranch and at the art gallery and keeping up with your own art?"

"Yes, I am, it's a dumb idea."

She nodded. "Just like the art gallery."

He nodded, then sent her a sly look. "But intriguing just the same."

She had to admit he was right about that, but it was not at all practical. So best not to dwell on it, but she couldn't stop herself from taking a picture of both numbers, and some others of both businesses.

They just barely made it back to the ranch before dinner. Rachel wondered why it felt so familiar coming back to the ranch. It almost felt like home even though she'd only been there a short time. She decided it was just hunger.

CHAPTER 10

Adam frowned when Rachel came into the dining room laughing at something Tim had said. The two of them had been gone all day into town. Everyone said they were just friends and hung out because of their mutual artistic bents, but he wasn't sure he believed that. They looked too cozy for that type of relationship. Her eyes were sparkling with mirth and he was grinning at her with sappy puppy dog eyes. Adam felt like barfing, but his mother would not appreciate that at the dinner table, so he looked around to find something else to focus on.

The Jeffersons' and the Kiplings' had melded during the day. The two sets of twins were having an uproarious discussion about twin pranks to pull on teachers and other unsuspecting victims. Emma had let Beth hang out with her and Tony and it looked like Alyssa's spot as Tony's favorite had been usurped by her younger sister. Both sets of parents and his grandfather had spent the day riding the land and talking about ranch differences, then cooking up a huge meal for the nineteen of them.

It was all one big happy family it seemed. The dining

room table had all the leaves in it and they still had to use a folding table, that the twin sets had commandeered.

Rachel slid into her chair. “I hope we didn’t hold you up.”

His mother smiled at Rachel. “Not at all dear, you’re right on time. Did you and Tim have a pleasant time in town?”

Tim nodded. “We did, it’s a cute little town and we even managed to get the candy order right, I think. Katie helped us with it. She was very supportive.”

Adam noticed the twins perk up at that. Cade grinned. “Katie’s the best. Chase and I have been friends with her forever.”

Tim nodded. “She’s a little cutie, too.”

Rachel elbowed him. “You, sir, are too young for her. You’re just a baby in her eyes.”

“Am not.”

“Are too. She’s at least three years older,” Rachel said.

“Meh, three years is nothing.”

Chase piped up, “Sounds like cradle robbing to me. Don’t think she’s into younger guys.”

Cade laughed. “Unless it’s Tony.”

Tony clapped his hands “Me, me, me.”

Everyone laughed and started passing the food. But Adam noticed both Chase and Tim looked a little tense.

Rachel elbowed Tim and handed him a bowl of potatoes. She gave him a look that made Tim chuckle and shake his head. Adam wondered what that was all about. Rachel and Tim clearly had secrets, or some kind of intimate communication going on. As Adam filled his plate he wondered why that bothered him. He didn’t think Tim was dangerous or a bad guy, in any way. So why didn’t he want Rachel to spend so much time with him? And why would Adam care if they had secrets? It was a ridiculous reaction. It’s not like it was jealousy or anything like that.

Adam was clearly too old for Rachel, he needed a mature

wife that would be able to stand beside him and help shepherd his younger siblings. He was the oldest and that came with a lot of responsibility. He had a duty to make sure all his siblings did well and made sound choices. He'd already tried to warn Beau about marrying a woman so young, but he'd been soundly ignored.

But he wasn't about to make the same error in judgment. He had to carry the burdens of the first born, and that did not leave room for dalliances with women nearly ten years his junior. It was fine for Beau to be foolish, but Adam did not have that luxury. Of course, he knew all this, so there was no reason for him to dislike the relationship between Tim and Rachel. He needed to remember she was just a girl and treat her like a younger sister. Just like Emma. He looked at Emma and then back at Rachel. Treat them the same? He could certainly do that. Couldn't he?

~

RACHEL WONDERED what Adam was brooding about, he hadn't said a word all evening. He sure was a grumpy guy. She hoped there wasn't something wrong that he didn't want to say. The guy needed to lighten up a bit, he didn't have to carry the whole world on his shoulders. But he did seem to be doing that about half the time if not more. She'd never known a guy that took his responsibilities to the extreme that Adam did. It was admirable, she supposed, but she wondered if it wasn't a little on the obsessive side, the guy needed to chill out once in a while and simply enjoy life.

She wanted to get his attention off whatever he was brooding about. But she couldn't think of a way to do so. Maybe she could ask him about the miniature golf course, Tim might not like that, but she was more concerned with distracting Adam than Tim's feelings.

Deciding to throw Tim under the bus she said, "Tim and I saw the abandoned mini-golf place, it's very cute. Adam, do you have any idea what it would cost to buy something like that and restore it? Tim was curious about it and since you're the financial guy in the family, I thought you might have an opinion."

Adam frowned. "I really have no idea."

Hank looked at Tim with raised eyebrows.

Tim flushed. "It was just a silly conversation, there were two for sale places and Rachel and I were just imagining buying them and reopening them. I felt sorry for the mini golf place, it's been abandoned. The fun wooden constructs are decaying and need some TLC."

Ellen said, "That's not exactly your bailiwick."

Tim nodded. "Yeah, but Terry would be in hog heaven helping me to restore them. Not that I'm planning to do that. I'm pretty busy between working on the ranch and the art gallery and making my sculptures."

Hank cleared his throat. "Tim, I love having you work the ranch and you are always welcome to stay and do that. For the rest of your life, if you want to. But if your heart is calling you elsewhere, I have no intention of holding you back. I love you and want you to find your place in life, and if that's not on the ranch, then that's okay with me."

"Thanks, Dad." Tim cleared his throat. "I don't have any place else I want to be right now. But it's nice to know I have your blessing, if that changes."

Hank nodded and Ellen took his hand and squeezed it.

Tim looked at Rachel. "Trouble maker."

Rachel hadn't thought through the consequences of her mouthing off and now felt really bad about it. "I'm sorry, I didn't mean anything. Just livening up the conversation."

Adam shook his head. "That you did, little girl, that you did."

Tim said, "We could talk about the photo studio. That's the other one for sale. And all the things you talked about doing, Rachel."

Rachel shook her head. "I'm sure we can think of something else to talk about."

Alyssa said, "So about my graduation the day after tomorrow. What's the plan?"

Rachel was so glad Alyssa was changing the subject she could have kissed her. As everyone discussed transportation over the mountains Rachel thought about her foolish comment. She had indeed acted like a little girl, with no real forethought to what can of worms she was opening. She would have died if someone had said that to her family, and gotten everyone riled up for no good reason. What a fool she was. She wanted to crawl into her bed, pull the covers over her head and not come out for a month or two—or at least until all the Jeffersons went home.

She looked over at Tim and he winked at her, so she assumed she was forgiven.

CHAPTER 11

Rachel was loading her equipment into Tim's truck. He'd forgiven her for her faux pas at dinner the other night and had teased her mercilessly the next day. She'd taken it with good grace for about six hours. Then had punched him in the stomach and told him to knock it off. He'd laughed like crazy. Telling her he was just waiting for her to get over feeling bad.

She was taking nearly every piece of her equipment because she just didn't know what she would want to take pictures of in Fort Collins, at Alyssa's graduation from the Colorado State University. She'd probably have to ride back with one of the Kiplings since she didn't think Tim was coming all the way back to Spirit Lake before heading home to Washington. They would be driving back down for the wedding in a couple of months anyway, so it made sense to leave after graduation for the two-day drive back to Washington. Fort Collins was between Spirit Lake and Chedwick so it didn't make sense to drive all the way back.

She was staying to help Alyssa plan the wedding. Since it was going to be so soon, they would have to hustle to get it together in time. Fortunately, the Kiplings belonged to a church in town that was very picturesque, and the pastor was happy to perform the ceremony. So, the ceremony was good, all they had to worry about was the invitations and the dress and the attendant's clothing and the decorations and the flowers and the rehearsal dinner and the wedding reception. Piece of cake, oh yeah and the cake.

But first, before they got crazy with all that, was graduation. Could Alyssa cram anything else into such a short time? Rachel didn't think so, but she wasn't going to mention it just in case it sounded like a challenge. Because Alyssa liked nothing better than a challenge.

"Anything else you're going to cram in my ride?" Tim asked, as she set her last tripod on the floor of the back seat. Fortunately, he had an extended cab truck, so she didn't have to put it in the bed.

"Nope, I think I'm good."

"Alrighty then, let's hook up the horse trailer and we'll be ready to roll."

So, he definitely wasn't coming back after graduation. She wondered who she could ride back with. Alyssa probably had it all planned out from dinner the other night. She'd been too mortified by her actions to listen to the discussion, so she had no idea what the plan was.

There was quite the caravan leaving the ranch, heading for Fort Collins. Both families totaled eighteen people plus her made nineteen, how Alyssa had managed to get tickets for all of them to attend she didn't know, but she had. They had seven vehicles total. All of them extended cab pickups and one pulling a horse trailer.

The drive to Fort Collins took about three and a half hours. Rachel had her camera in her lap the whole time and occasionally took pictures out the window of the truck. She'd been doing the driving when she came into Colorado and over the mountains, so she'd had to pull over for any pictures she couldn't live without. Which had been more than a normal person, but not nearly as many as she would have liked. She loved the view of Denver when they dropped down out of the mountains, came around a corner on I-70 and it spread out before them.

Tim laughed as she took picture after picture. "It's a city, what's the big deal?"

"It's so big and look at that perfectly straight street. It looks like it runs straight into down town. I've never seen anything like it."

Tim looked at her like she was an idiot. "That's because you live in a tiny town tucked in between the mountains and the lake. Out here there is lots of land and very few natural formations to go around. So why not have straight streets?"

"I need to come explore Denver before I go back home. Maybe Alyssa and I can do some wedding shopping."

"I'm sure she would be more than happy to spend Dad's money on frou frou stuff," Tim said dryly.

"Goody."

ADAM COULDN'T BELIEVE how many times Tim Jefferson pulled his truck to the side of the road or slowed down, as Rachel leaned out the window with her camera in her hand. He was ready to go slap both of them. But he supposed that was the payment for having her in his truck. An artist through and through. He supposed Tim didn't mind so much, since he was also an artist. Although his carving wood statues, was not the same as Rachel taking a picture of every damn thing. He was surprised that it hadn't added more time to the drive than it had, only about twenty minutes.

They had plenty of time, they'd left early, and Alyssa's

graduation wasn't until one. So, there was more than enough time for her to graduate and them to drive back before it got dark. The days were long this time of year.

Alyssa had talked about taking Trail Ridge Road through the Rocky Mountain National Park, on the way back from graduation. With the dry weather they'd had this winter it might even be open. He supposed if they did find out it was open early this year, Rachel would want to go that route also. It was a spectacular drive and would only add a few minutes, due to the slower speed because of the narrowness of the road and the many switchbacks. But it was the shortest route by far. It was touted as the highest paved road in America and in places it had a sharp drop off.

Drew interrupted his musings. "So, what do you think that drone is doing?"

Adam sighed. "I've wracked my brain over that question. If we had any idea where it was coming from or going to that might help. It just appears and then is gone until the next time. No warning, and it's so startling it's hard to remember to watch where it goes." He'd been disgusted with himself when he hadn't paid attention to where the drone had gone when he'd been confronted with it.

"Do you think it has something to do with that pickax Thomas found?"

"It doesn't seem likely, but then again they are both rather odd things to be happening, so maybe they are."

"If someone thinks something is buried on our land they might be scouting it out with the drone and digging with the pickax." Drew shrugged.

"Thomas did say the pickax was stuck pretty hard into some rock. Maybe they were digging for treasure." Adam guffawed. "Stupid place to dig if you ask me."

Drew grinned. "You got that right, that land is all bedrock, which is why we don't plant there. Dumb asses."

"Yeah, down by the river would be a better place to dig, not that I think they're going to find any treasure buried anywhere. There are some tall tales about gold and money going missing further north."

"Yeah, the gold from Soda Creek up in the Never Summer Range, or maybe they think one of the Gilpin county thefts made its way over to our land." Drew smirked.

"Ha, or maybe they think Elk mountain is the same as the Gore mountain range and are looking for the lost gold mine."

"They wouldn't be off by much, only fifty miles or so," Drew said with an exaggerated shrug.

Adam laughed. "As the crow flies."

"Same, same."

"Riiiight."

As Drew answered a text, Adam had to wonder if it was something silly like that, because he couldn't think of any other idea that would fit the odd circumstances. He turned it over in his mind as he drove.

They had lunch at a place not too far from Fort Collins called Wholly Stromboli, it was Italian food and Adam had to admit it was delicious. Adam wasn't sure how Alyssa had found the place originally, since it was about an hour from Fort Collins. But she seemed to know some of the people running it, so she had clearly been there more than a few times.

Rachel had her camera out the whole time they were in the restaurant taking pictures of all of them, and the food, and God only knew what all. How she managed to eat her lunch was beyond him, but when they got up to leave, her plate was clean.

The woman was a menace with that camera. But no one else seemed to mind her snapping picture after picture. He resigned himself to that being the way the whole day would be.

CHAPTER 12

Rachel dragged all her camera equipment out of Tim's truck and handed nearly half of it to the man. She'd decided he was her designated pack mule. When she told him, he was now Tim-the-pack-mule, he grinned and brayed loud enough to draw everyone's attention and then laughed his fool head off, when she turned bright red. Alyssa just rolled her eyes at him and started off toward the graduation venue.

Adam walked up. "Did you bring everything you owned?"

"Nearly, I don't know what kind of pictures Alyssa wants or what the lighting will be like or how far away we'll be, so yes, I brought nearly everything, except the light boxes."

"I can help carry if you want," Adam said.

Rachel grinned at him, she had no intention of turning down help, the less she had to carry the easier it was to stay focused on the actual photography. "Awesome."

Tim patted Adam on the back. "You are going to regret offering to help, my friend. She takes it as a lifelong commitment. But I'm happy to have a fellow pack mule."

Adam raised one eyebrow. "Lifelong? How long have you been toting and carrying?"

Tim shook his head sadly. "She got her first camera when she was about eight I think, but she didn't need much help back then. In fact, no one was allowed to touch it or even breathe near it. But then she started acquiring more and more and more crap. So about ten years."

Rachel rolled her eyes. "I didn't get tripods or extra lenses or anything for you to carry, until I hit sixteen, and started taking pictures for the school newspaper. So, it couldn't have been any longer than six years, drama queen."

Tim put his hands on his hips. "Drama king. Thank you very much."

"Enough of your silliness, Tim Jefferson, we need to catch up with Alyssa. Thanks for your help, Adam."

"Hey, I'm helping too," Tim whined.

"Yes, you are, but A, you're complaining about it, B, it's your sister that I'm taking pictures of, and C, I've known you since birth. But I still do appreciate the help. Now let's move it." She started off at a fast clip to follow Alyssa and the rest of the family that were a couple dozen yards ahead of them. But she still heard Tim muttering about bossy women and Adam chuckling at him.

She hoped having Adam near and at her disposal wouldn't distract her too much. She was normally able to tune out everyone when she was in the photographer zone, but Adam was a force of nature she'd never encountered. With his rugged good looks and dark curly hair, she loved that he was so tall. And did she mention he smelled good, too? Yeah, the man was walking distraction. If he had a better personality she would be all over him. Fortunately for her and her peace of mind, he was kind of grumpy. She'd seen him nearly pleasant a few times, but he always held back from entering into the chaos and fun that surrounded both families.

She loved that chaos, most of the time anyway. Growing up, as an only child, could be lonely. So, she'd always enjoyed going to Alyssa's house where she had surrogate siblings. And at the end of the day, she could also go back home, to her quiet life. When they all got to be too much for her.

~

ADAM WATCHED Rachel charge after Alyssa, she moved with a feminine grace that was poetry in motion. Her legs ate up the ground and her hair flew behind her. He tried not to make it obvious he was staring. But he saw Tim look at him, then look at Rachel and smirk.

Tim chuckled. "You and every other living breathing man, my friend."

Adam just ignored the remark and kept walking. He had no intention of giving Tim any more ammunition than he already had. Plus, he had no intention of going after her, so it was a moot point. But he could admit to himself that she drew every one of his mating instincts to the forefront, and he had to fight to keep from imagining her wrapped around him in every way.

Alyssa's graduation was like all other graduations he'd ever attended. A bunch of people pontificating on the amazing lives the graduates had spread out before them. The best part of the whole thing was that the class was relatively small since it was just the biomedical sciences and veterinary school graduating. So, the diploma ceremony was quick. Rachel switched between her zoom lens and the telephoto taking pictures of the whole class and the stage and even some of the crowd.

Alyssa looked to be quite popular with her class as

everyone came to get their picture taken with her. Rachel was patiently taking all the pictures and promised to send each person a copy. How she was going to manage to get all their emails he didn't know. But maybe Alyssa already had them or there was a class mailing list or something. He was proud of Beau when he didn't get jealous over the number of males in her class that wanted pictures with Alyssa.

Once all the festivities were over the Jeffersons' kissed Alyssa goodbye and headed off for home. Alyssa started to look distressed at their leaving. He noticed Rachel tried to help by asking Alyssa what she wanted pictures of across the campus. That did help, and Beau had stories and anecdotes about those same locations from when he'd been a student. Finally, they'd taken pictures of everything and were ready to get on the road.

CHAPTER 13

How in the hell had he drawn the short straw to drive Rachel through Rocky Mountain National Park? For fuck's sake, he'd just spent the last two hours toting all her crap around as she took zillions of graduation, family, friends, and campus pictures. Now he was going to be spending the next three to four hours with her. Just the two of them alone in his truck. Her closeness and scent were driving him crazy. They would have to converse and he had no idea what they could talk about for that long.

It was because of all the camera crap she'd brought with her. It took up over half of the backseat, which was why she couldn't ride with Beau and Alyssa because Beau's back seat was already half-filled with Alyssa's graduation gifts and clothes. Drew, the traitor, had laughed, slapped him on the back and gotten in Cade's truck with Chase and Grandpa K, saying he had to go to work in the morning so needed his beauty sleep.

Rachel would probably want to stop at every turn out and rest stop to take a zillion more pictures. This was confirmed when she took the memory card out of her camera, wrote *Graduation* on it and put a fresh, new one in the camera. He groaned inwardly.

"I'm so glad the road is open. Alyssa's been wanting to take this drive through the park since her first day on campus, but with it only being open the few summer months when she came back home to see all of us, she's never had the chance."

Adam nodded. She squirmed in her seat and he didn't know if she was excited or nervous.

"I'm thrilled to have the chance. I'll try not to drive you too crazy stopping every five minutes. But this might be my only chance to drive through the park without actually driving it myself, which means I can really look to see what a good shot would be."

Now he felt like a jerk, for dreading this. "You are welcome to stop as much as you like we've got a good five hours of daylight left, so we should have plenty of time even with stopping in Estes Park for some dinner. As long as we're out of the park by dark we'll be fine."

She beamed at him and her hazel eyes sparkled with excitement. "I really, really appreciate it, Adam. And will owe you one. A big one."

His mind went straight to the gutter on how she could repay him. All of them involving some sort of nakedness. He shifted in his seat to hide his reaction and cleared his throat. "No payment necessary."

"I'll think of something."

He didn't let his mind go anywhere with that statement. He kept his eyes on the road like it was the hardest drive on earth, when, in fact, he was following Beau down a nearly deserted highway. Since Beau had gone to CSU for eight years to earn his Doctor of Veterinary Medicine, he knew the best way to, and from their home, both through the park and not.

"You know I was thinking about that drone that keeps showing up," Rachel said.

He grunted.

"Well if you really want to find it you could set up some motion-activated cameras."

He turned his head and looked at her for a moment.

She stumbled on, "If you put them up above the height the cattle would turn them on, and point them at the six to eight-foot level, you might be able to see where it's coming onto your land. I know it's a lot of ground to cover, but maybe you could rent some, or I don't know… it was just a thought." She folded her arms and looked out the window.

As he turned the idea over in his mind, he saw her tense up even from his peripheral vision. "That's actually not a bad idea."

She looked back so quick her hair snapped. "You think so?"

"I do, it would take some investigation, and planning but it's the best idea I've heard so far."

She smiled so wide, the joy filled the truck. "I thought you thought I was an idiot mentioning it. You have so much land and cameras are not cheap, and I don't know what resources—"

"It's okay Rachel. I needed to think about it for a minute. Have you already researched this idea?"

"Well I might have looked at things online, a bit."

He chuckled at her expression of pride mixed with anxiety as she continued on. "There are a lot of different options. Many remote cameras are used for hunting. The problem is they don't have a very long range, so you would need a lot of them. The ones I saw online have about a sixty-five-foot trigger distance and a one-hundred-and-twenty-degree wide angle sensor, for about eighty dollars. You would need a couple hundred of them to cover your perimeter."

"True, but we could do a portion of the land at a time, it wouldn't have to be the whole thing done at once. Maybe do a quarter at a time, for two weeks then move them. I think we could see what direction the drone is coming from and then investigate from there. Once we didn't need them anymore we could probably sell them to hunters at half the price and not be out a ton of money. I'll talk to my dad about the idea."

She looked so pleased with herself for having a good idea he nearly laughed out loud.

~

RACHEL WAS SO THRILLED Adam hadn't treated her like an idiot and really was considering her idea. She'd been freaked out when she'd realized he was the one that would be driving her back to their ranch. The two of them in his truck alone for several hours seemed like torture of the highest form. He'd been very helpful with toting around all her equipment at graduation, but she always still felt like he was indulging her, and he really thought she was an inconvenience.

She'd gotten that idea stuck in her head the very first minute she'd met him, and she hadn't been able to shake it. So, when he said her idea was a good one it had relieved a lot of anxiety. When he was being nice he was so darn attractive, she wanted to jump him. It had been a while since she'd had anyone she was remotely interested in that way. She lived in such a small town there just weren't that many prospects. But that didn't account for the crazy attraction she felt for

Adam. Chase, Cade and Drew were also very attractive men and she didn't feel anything toward them. There were also a couple of the hired hands that were cuties, but again no interest at all. Just this big cowboy with a grumpy attitude.

She entertained herself with ideas of where they could get naked. Not the truck, vehicles were just not that comfortable, at least not the front seat. If all her crap was not in the back it might work, but the seat was still pretty narrow. She looked out the window at a pretty meadow, that might be good, but it was too close to the road. An old barn came into view. Now that would work, it was falling down and weathered, but maybe behind it.

The truck started slowing down and over to the side of the road. *Crap did I say that out loud? Can he read my mind?*

She looked up. "W-why are we stopping?"

"I thought you might want to take some pictures, you were staring at that old barn pretty hard. Alyssa must have thought so too, because they are stopped up ahead." He waved his hand toward Beau's truck.

She looked and saw Beau's truck pulled onto the shoulder of the road about fifty yards ahead. Her cheeks flamed, and she fumbled with her seat belt. Nearly dropping her camera as she stumbled out of the cab. "Oh yes, of course, it's a very cool structure it would make a terrific study. Be right back."

The man was going to think she was a complete idiot. He'd told her she could stop any time and apparently Alyssa was looking out for her, too. If she hadn't been having hot fantasies, she would have noticed it and *wanted* to take pictures. God, she had to get herself under control, immediately if not sooner.

She took a few pictures just for form, but her heart wasn't in it and she knew they wouldn't be that great, she tried to settle down and get some good ones, but she was too rattled.

She got back in the truck and smiled sweetly. “Thanks for stopping.”

“No prob. Just let me know if you see something you like.” He shrugged and started up the truck.

She saw something she liked, all right, but it had nothing to do with photography.

CHAPTER 14

Adam wasn't sure what had rattled Rachel, but she'd acted like a snake was going to bite her when he'd pulled off the road. She'd nearly dropped her camera trying to get out of the cab. He had no idea what was wrong with her. Women were a mystery. Maybe he should bring up a subject to talk about, so he didn't seem so scary to her. But what?

Ah, Beau's project might be just the thing. "So, has Beau talked to you about taking some pictures for his presentation?"

She startled and then nodded. "He has, but he's not sure when he'll be able to take me out to find each of the heifers and their calves. With the wedding in two months, Alyssa and I are going to be crazy trying to get everything planned."

It was just a wedding, what was the big deal? A dress, some cake, some food and invitations. Seemed pretty straight forward to him. He knew they were planning to have the ceremony at their church and they could always use the Grange Hall for the reception if they wanted. He wasn't about to make light of the whole thing though because he didn't want to downplay the work involved.

He nodded. "You can always stay a few days after the wedding furor dies down, one of us can help you find the right livestock. In fact, some photographic documentation of the herd might be a good idea. Not sure if we would want all the animals photographed, but some of the ones we might want to show would be good, or any of the young bulls we might want to sell. I imagine our website could use some new pictures also. It's been a while since it was updated. It might be a couple of week's work. We would be happy to pay you for your time and expertise."

"Thanks, I'll keep that in mind. I've been toying with the idea of going to art school, but I haven't really decided yet."

"Where are you thinking about attending?"

"There are several Art Institutes, Seattle, Denver, then there are a couple of great schools in California, New York and Florida. I'm not sure I want to get as far away from home as New York or Florida. I've put in a couple of applications, so we'll see what happens."

"So, are you looking at a bachelor's degree or masters?"

"I don't know for sure. I've taken a lot of online classes and learned a lot. But Alyssa insists that a hands-on full-time college is best."

"The two are very different experiences, but I don't know that one is actually better than the other. It's more what options will best fit into your life style. I went away to college for my business degree and then took online courses to continue my education."

She laughed, and the sound shivered through him. "I've done just the opposite, started online, and may finish up going away."

He followed Beau into Estes Park and the parking lot where all the elk gathered. He was certain she would want pictures. There were hundreds of Elk that hung out in Estes Park, sometimes they were a nuisance. It was such a large herd that everyone was always floored by them.

"Wow, look at all the elk. Are we stopping so I can photograph them?"

"I can't imagine any other reason to be stopping here, have fun, but don't get too close. They might hang out in town, but they are still wild animals."

She frowned at him.

"No, I don't think you're an idiot, but people try it every year. Sometimes total idiots try to put a child up on one of their backs for a photo."

"You're joking, that's ridiculous. And dangerous." She shuddered.

"I wish I was joking. Come on, I could use a stretch of my legs."

"Oh, in that case can you grab the tripod, and the green bag with the extra lenses?"

"Yes, ma'am, whatever you say, ma'am."

She got out of the cab laughing, as Alyssa came over to her. He shivered and got her equipment out of the back seat and heard Beau walk up.

"Gonna tote and carry again for the little miss?" Beau asked.

"Somebody's gotta."

"I suppose. Do you think they'll be long?" Beau asked. "I was thinking we could grab an early dinner here in town and then we wouldn't be starving if it takes us all night driving through the park."

"Sounds like an excellent idea."

~

RACHEL AND ALYSSA headed toward the animals, they weren't

going to get too close. But it was amazing to see so many wild animals just standing in a field, practically in the middle of town.

Alyssa joined her arm with Rachel as they had done for years and years. God, she was going to miss her friend when she left Colorado.

Alyssa said quietly. "So, you were laughing when you got out of the truck. Are you doing okay with Adam? I know he can be unfriendly."

Rachel glanced over her shoulder and noticed the guys were back a few yards. "Actually, it's going much better than I envisioned. We've had a companionable drive. He said to let him know if I want to stop somewhere for pictures. But you've already set that precedence."

Alyssa laughed. "I've been trying to anticipate you."

"Well, it's working fine." They stopped at a place that would give her a good view of the animals, but was a safe distance away.

Adam and Beau joined them.

She took the tripod from Adam's hand and set it up, swapped out her wide-angle lens for the telephoto and mounted it. There was a small elk family off to one side the bull, cow and calf. She quickly snapped pictures of the family group since that sight was not a norm for elk, who primarily stay in single sex herds, so it was a treat not to be missed. Not much about this giant herd was consistent with typical behavior however. There were a number of very pregnant cows moving slowly and Rachel wondered how soon they would deliver.

When she had plenty of pictures of elk, they loaded into the trucks and went in search of food, they decided on barbeque. The restaurant wasn't quite in town, but it was on one of the access roads to the national park. Since it was a little early for dinner they didn't have the wait they normally would.

When they were seated at the table they looked over the menu. Rachel asked the guys, "What's good?"

Beau said, "Pretty much everything is delicious."

Adam nodded. "But they are kind of famous for their pulled pork sandwiches."

"Perfect, I love pulled pork." Rachel snapped her menu closed and set it on the table. She hated trying to decide what to order at a new restaurant.

Alyssa gasped. "Oh my God, did you see the appetizers? I want one of each they sound delicious. Oh, wait they have a combo that has them all, we have to get that. Please, pretty please."

Beau laughed. "Of course, we can order it. Are you going to have anything else?"

Alyssa nodded. "I should order a salad. But that trout sounds too good. I have to try it."

"We're going to end up taking a lot of left overs with us. They have generous portions," Adam said.

"Oh, goody, car snacks." Alyssa smacked her lips.

Beau laughed and Adam groaned. Rachel rolled her eyes, she never could figure out where Alyssa put all the food. She'd known her since they were kids and Alyssa always packed it away while most people ate about half the amount.

CHAPTER 15

After they ordered, while they waited for the appetizers, Alyssa said, "So since it's the four of us and graduation is over, can we talk about the wedding? Adam you're going to be Beau's best man and Rachel is my maid of honor. So, there's a couple of things we need to talk about."

Rachel looked at the guys and they looked like deer in headlights. Alyssa laughed. "It won't be that bad, but you need to know what your respective roles are."

Beau said, "Showing up in nice clothes?"

Adam chuckled. "My job is to make sure he doesn't pass out."

Alyssa nodded. "Both true, but there are a couple more things you need to do. I want to have Tony be the ring bearer, so Adam if you can handle him when he gets to the front, until we get to the ring part that would be helpful. After we've gotten the rings he can go sit down."

"Sure, no problem."

"You'll also be Rachel's escort down the aisle afterwards

and the two of you can drive us from the church to the reception."

"I can handle that also. Are you planning on using the Grange for the reception?"

"We can, but I've also been thinking about having a party at the ranch, outside under the stars."

Beau patted her hand. "You know it won't be dark until nearly eight thirty, that time of year. I thought we were talking about a three o'clock wedding. That would be a very long party to last until the stars came out."

"True, we probably need to talk about that more, Beau. I know we've got the Grange on hold and we would need to find out what all would be needed to have it at the ranch, anyway."

Rachel said, "It would probably be a lot easier to have it at the Grange. If you have it at the ranch, you'll have to get tables and chairs and set up some kind of dance floor. And somewhere to cater the food."

"Yeah and the ranch is kind of smelly for people who don't live on one. We're all used to it, but there are other people who are not." Adam shrugged.

"I'm not sure I care that much about other people, both of us are from ranching families." Alyssa waved her hand. "So, all of our closest people would be fine. Anyway, I'll give it some more thought. Adam as the best man you'll need to give the first toast. Both fathers will probably do the same and if Grandpa K wants to he's welcome."

"Okaaay, I can think of something brilliant to say." Adam frowned, clearly trying to think of what to say.

"Rachel, you can take a few pics at the rehearsal if you want, but I'm going to need to find a photographer for the event. I need you by my side."

Rachel gave her best friend a smile. "I understand, it might make me a little crazy not to be behind the camera, but

I'll do my best. How many people do you think will come from Chedwick?"

Alyssa said, "I'm not really expecting anyone but my family. I'm sending invitations to everyone, but I'll tell them we'll have a reception in town after breeding season. Maybe October."

Rachel wasn't so sure about that. Alyssa was a favorite around town, but she'd wait to see what happened. It wouldn't surprise her if half the town made the journey. The October reception would be packed.

Before anything else could be said the appetizers arrived and they all dug in tasting them. The meals came right after that. They had enough food for an army. Rachel decided the pulled pork sandwich was the best she'd ever eaten, but she'd had too many appetizers so only got through about half her sandwich and a handful of the fries. The coleslaw was good too, but she only had a few bites.

She tried to wait patiently for everyone to eat their fill, but wasn't terribly successful. She wanted to get on the road. There were pictures to be taken and places to explore.

Finally, Alyssa looked at her and said, "Okay Miss Ants in the Pants we can go. As soon as we get the rest of this food in a doggy bag."

Rachel grinned. "You mean an Alyssa bag?"

"Yes, I do, except for your cold French fries. You can take those with you."

"Gladly."

Beau and Adam both looked at her with identical expressions of horror. "Yes. I know I'm weird, but I love cold fries almost as much as the hot ones. So, I will be taking them with me, since I ate too many appetizers to eat one of my favorite foods."

Adam and Beau shuddered.

The waitress brought some large to go containers so

Alyssa and Rachel started divvying up the food. One container per truck. Beau watched the proceedings and corrected them on the brothers' preferences while Adam paid the bill.

They left the restaurant and headed into the park.

~

ADAM DROVE ON AUTO PILOT, he was still thinking about what he would say as the best man. How could he give a toast when he still wasn't sure Beau was making the right decision? Yes, he seemed happy with Alyssa and she with him, but was it really going to last? He supposed it could. They did have a lot in common. Similar families and values, lifestyle and careers. When they worked together as vets it was like they read each other's mind. He'd watched Alyssa anticipate Beau and hand him things before he even asked.

Maybe they truly were a match made in heaven. He wished he could be as care free as Beau was. Beau didn't analyze everything to death like he did. Beau took life by the horns and hung on for the ride. Adam wasn't sure he could ever be that way. He thought about everything, and how every decision would affect everyone else. Maybe he should take a lesson from his younger brother.

As far as the toast went, he could talk about how compatible they were. That would be easy. He'd need to think about that more. He should put it away for this drive over Trail Ridge, it could be a treacherous road and he needed to be paying attention. He saw Beau pull to the side in an overlook area and followed him, so Rachel could take pictures. Alyssa seemed to know what Rachel would want to take pictures of before Rachel could say anything to him. Almost like sisters.

He stopped, and Rachel swapped out her telephoto lens for her wide angle and started snapping pictures. They were still near the base of the mountains and he knew the girls would both be in awe, up higher where the tree growth stopped, and the views went on and on for miles.

Beau must have been thinking the same thing. He said, "This is just the beginning, trust me you'll want more time up higher."

Rachel looked at Beau and then at Adam who nodded. She said, "Well let's get moving then. I don't want to miss the best part."

She took a few more pictures and then hurried back to the truck. She jumped in the truck and fastened her seat belt. "So, what's so cool up higher, isn't it the same?"

He shook his head. "Not at all, we'll hit timberline and then it will all change."

"What do you mean by timberline?"

"Trees can't grow above a certain altitude. When we hit that it will look like a ruler was drawn along the mountains and they will be bare of all growth above that line, except for the sturdiest brush and grasses. It might be too early for the flowers that grow in all colors. You'll see, it's quite interesting."

She looked skeptical. "I'll have to take your word for that, it sounds rather odd to me."

"It is odd, but once we hit that elevation, which if I remember correctly is a bit over eleven thousand feet, you can see for miles. No trees or anything to block the view. At the very top you can see across the whole mountain range. It's spectacular."

"Cool."

Adam said, "You might want to take another day and really explore the park while you're here. This drive takes you through the park but there are lots of trails to walk on. There's also the Old Fall River Road that's about nine miles long. It's one way because it so narrow, but you might like going on that, too. You could easily spend a whole day exploring and not venture too far into the park."

"I'm not sure I'll have time for any of that. I think Alyssa is going to be keeping me busy with wedding preparations." She sighed. "Speaking of which, there is one other thing that you and I need to do."

Something else? He hoped it was something simple. "What's that?"

"Decorate whatever vehicle their driving to the airport."

Adam guffawed. "Like soap the windows and tie cans to the back of the car."

She nodded. "Something like that, but it needs to be done so they can see to drive to the airport, and also be festive enough to draw attention."

"I see what you mean. I don't think anyone would appreciate cans and shoes bumping along the road on I-70. They might go flying off and hit the car behind them." He could imagine a shoe or can winging into someone's windshield at sixty miles an hour, startling the driver and causing an accident, maybe even breaking a windshield.

"Exactly, but a big *Just Married* sign securely fastened to the tail gate would be fun."

"Okay, let me give it some thought. They're pulling off at another overlook." He pulled in next to them.

Rachel hopped out of the car and shivered. "It's colder here."

Beau nodded. "It'll be even colder up higher and there is often a breeze. There can be a thirty-degree difference from town to the summit, without the wind chill."

Rachel frowned and shivered again. "I didn't bring a coat, it never occurred to me I would need one."

Adam walked up and handed her a jacket. "I keep a couple in the truck for times like these. It will be too big on you, but it will keep you warm."

"Thanks."

Alyssa came around the front of Beau's truck also in a coat too big for her. Rachel at least had more height to carry it off, Alyssa looked like a little kid in Beau's jacket. "Well don't we look like fashionistas?" Rachel laughed.

Alyssa grinned. "Better than being frozen."

Beau said. "Let's get to picture taking ladies, we've still got forty miles of road to cover."

Alyssa rolled her eyes. "And three hours to do it in. We could probably walk in that length of time."

"But you wouldn't have any time for picture taking," Beau said gravely. "And there isn't a lot of oxygen at this altitude, so you'd be huffing and puffing."

"I was being sarcastic," Alyssa said.

Beau nodded. "I'm aware."

Adam crossed his arms. "But there is something to be said for expedience, this park is amazing and I'm sure Rachel could spend three hours taking pictures before we even reached the summit, let alone the continental divide."

"Yeah, you're probably right, Adam. She does like to take lots of pictures. But they do turn out beautiful." Alyssa shrugged like that's all that mattered.

Adam agreed that she took great pictures, but there was a lot to explore and he didn't want to be on the road after dark. That would be dangerous, many of the stretches had no guard rails. "I'm sure they do. But we don't want her to miss anything because it gets dark. This isn't a fun road to drive at night."

Alyssa frowned. "I can see that. Rachel, let's get a move on."

CHAPTER 16

"One last shot." Rachel switched out her wide-angle lens for one that could take closeups. There was the cutest little plant popping out of the ground. She focused in on it and took half a dozen pictures at each shutter speed and focus point. When she was finished she stood up and noticed the three of them looking at her. "What?"

Adam said, "Did you seriously just take a hundred pictures of that tiny bud, that's not even out of the ground yet?"

"Not quite that many, but yes, I did. And when you see what I do with them, I will expect the praise it will be due."

Adam looked back down at the speck of green and then looked back at her. "If you insist."

Alyssa and Beau looked at the tiny plant then back at each other, shrugged and started walking back to the trucks.

She looked back at the little bud and said, "I'll show them, you'll be a star. Now grow strong my little friend."

Adam shook his head at her. "You're crazy. You do know that, right?"

"Crazy like a fox, Adam."

She started toward the truck and heard him mutter something under his breath that might have been. "Fox my ass, loon is closer." She just grinned, the man would be eating his words when she finished with those pictures.

The rest of the drive was similar, they would stop at some point and she would take a bunch of pictures while they waited. Up above timberline it was as spectacular as Adam had said it would be. She literally could spend a whole day or two at that elevation. There were even some very brave animals popping their heads out of their burrows. Oh yes, at least two days.

When they got back into the truck after their stop at the continental divide she couldn't contain her excitement. "You are right it's amazing up here. To stand on the continental divide and realize all the rivers on your right flow into the Pacific Ocean and all the rivers on your left flow into the Atlantic Ocean, is kind of a cool thought." She continued, "It's so different from anything I've ever seen. And all those tiny plants and even some animals living up so high, it's amazing. Thank you so much for bringing me up."

He looked at her and a slow grin slid across his face. "It's been my pleasure to watch you. It's caused me to see things through your eyes. I'll be interested to see your finished pictures."

That smile changed his features from the stark expression he normally wore. He hardly looked like the same man and boy did she like what she saw. The smile softened his features and lit a spark in his eyes. Her fingers itched to take a picture of him, but she knew he wouldn't be appreciative of that idea, so she kept still. "It will be my pleasure to show them to you."

"Sounds good. We've got a couple more stops to make. We'll be coming upon the Colorado river soon. It runs fairly close to the road, but it doesn't look like much at this elevation, especially this year with the dry winter we had."

"But there's still plenty of snow," she said glancing around at all the snow on the ground.

"Not really, we can get thirty feet up here. Which is why the road is normally closed for another couple of weeks. These little piles you see are nothing."

"Wow that's a lot of snow." She'd never seen that much snow. About every five years they got dumped on for Christmas, but it was still only about three feet. Thirty feet was as tall as a house. That would be crazy to see.

"Yes, it is. Some years it doesn't open on Memorial Day because of the snowy road conditions. And there are occasions of freak storms in the summer that can cause the road to shut down until the snowplows can get it cleared and reopened. We don't drive it much… unless we have guests that want to see it."

She knew he was referring to her and Alyssa and it made her feel special that they had taken the time to drive them over the road. She leaned over the console and gave him a kiss on the cheek. She whispered, "Thanks."

His voice was gruff when he said, "You're welcome."

SHE'D JUST MEANT it as a thank you, but that little kiss on the cheek had sent fire racing through his blood. It was ridiculous if he thought about it, but his body didn't give a damn what his head had to say about it. He didn't know what to say or how to react, so he just kept driving.

What he wanted to do was stop the truck, drag her into his arms and kiss the living daylights out of her. Then if she was on board, strip her naked and bury himself in her. That's what he wanted to do, but it wasn't an option, so he just kept driving.

He cleared his throat. "There are a couple more turnouts left before we're off the mountain. There's still plenty of daylight to get out of the park, but we should probably finish up our exploration fairly soon. There might be deer or elk in the meadow just outside the park entrance in an hour or so as dusk settles. It's a popular place to see them in early morning or just before the sunset. It's not a huge herd like in Estes Park, but these won't be quite so domesticated either. And most of the time it's deer or even a moose on occasion."

"Oh, a moose would be fun to see."

"Yes, but they aren't sighted real often. Mainly it's a small herd of deer," Adam said.

"That would be fun, too. I'm not picky."

He laughed. "I noticed that when you took a bazillion pictures of the chipmunks."

"Chipmunks are cute."

"And the butterfly," he said dryly.

"Butterflies are beautiful."

He glanced at her. "It was a little white one."

"Still I liked it."

"And the lichen?"

She giggled. "Fine, you've made your point."

That giggle tore him up. "Anyway, the point being you need to be quick at the last couple stops if you want to see the deer." His voice had come out gruffer than he intended, and he saw her flinch. Dammit.

She said, "I'll keep that in mind." Then she turned to look out the window.

Now he'd pissed her off or hurt her feelings. He didn't know what to say so he said nothing and just drove. What an idiot he was.

When they got to the next turnout, she said, "No need to get out. I'll make it quick."

"Rachel, I didn't mean…"

"No, it's fine. I know I drew this trip out much longer than was necessary. You probably just want to get home and away from all of this. I'll be quick."

Now he'd ruined the trip for her and she felt bad. All because her giggle had set him on fire, with a lust he didn't want to feel for her. He sat in the truck thinking about how to fix it. Beau knocked on the window which startled him out of his thoughts. He powered the window down.

Beau said, "What's up? Rachel looks upset."

"I didn't mean anything by it. I just mentioned she might want to hurry if she wants to see the deer that hang out in the meadow after we exit the park."

"That makes sense, why would that upset her?"

Adam didn't want to admit he was abrupt with her because of his reaction to her laugh. "I think she took it as I'm tired of driving her around. It wasn't what I intended."

Beau's eyebrows lifted. "Of course not, you've always been a fan of driving. Since you were sixteen and got your first license."

"She doesn't know that."

Beau shrugged. "Tell her, dumbass."

"I'll try."

"What's this try shit. Do I need to start quoting Yoda at you?"

Adam rolled his eyes, and saw Rachel hurrying back to the truck. "I can handle it, asshole. Go back to your truck."

Rachel clambered in the cab and said tightly, "I hurried."

He sighed and didn't start the truck. He turned toward her. "Rachel, I didn't mean to make you feel bad or self-conscious. I don't mind driving you around. In fact, driving is something I enjoy. I just wanted you to be aware of the possibility of some pictures down lower. I didn't mean to sound gruff about it. Please don't let my attitude ruin your trip and photography."

"You're not sick of me and all my silly picture taking?"

He shook his head. "Not at all. I was attempting to tease you about that."

"It did sound like teasing at first. But then it changed."

He ran his hand behind his neck and looked up to see that Beau and Alyssa had left. Time to come clean. "It was your laugh."

"What's wrong with my laugh?"

"Nothing's wrong with it."

"Then what..."

In for a penny, in for a pound. "It made me want to stop in the middle of the road, drag you over the console and kiss the breath out of you. Then strip you naked and bury myself in you until next week."

"Oh...my... I had no idea."

He turned to start the truck. "Yeah, so I was a little agitated."

"Adam?"

"What?"

"I think I'd like that. Not in the middle of the road or where Beau and Alyssa would come to see where we were, but... All the rest sounds like a superior idea."

"It does?" He looked at her wondering if she really meant it.

"Yes, it does."

"I thought you didn't like me?"

She shrugged. "I don't always like you, in fact I rarely do." She shrugged again. "But what's that got to do with a good screw. Might relieve some tension."

He chuckled, she had to be the craziest woman he'd ever met.

She looked out the window. “But if we don’t want Beau and Alyssa coming back to see if we killed each other, we should probably drive.”

He sighed dramatically. “If we must.”

She giggled again, then gasped. “You didn’t tell Beau that, while I was taking pictures, did you?”

“Hell no. And stop giggling.” He put the truck in gear.

She giggled again. “I’ll try.”

“Woman.” He growled. Which sent her into peals of laughter, that made him grin despite himself and his inflamed body.

CHAPTER 17

Rachel undressed for bed and thought back over the day. Had Adam really meant what he'd said? She couldn't be sure because the rest of the drive had been spent companionably with no more mention of kissing or sex, which if she was honest was a little disappointing. They'd stopped a couple more times and though she didn't exactly hurry she didn't dawdle either. She was rewarded by seeing a half dozen mule deer feeding in the meadow, like Adam had mentioned, just outside the park entrance.

When they got back to the ranch Adam had helped her carry all the equipment to her room and then left. Which sucked because she'd been thinking maybe he would hang out and carry out some of the ideas he'd put in her head. Men were very strange.

She left her camera equipment packed. She didn't have the energy to look through the two memory cards she'd filled that day. She didn't feel like socializing with the family, even though it was only nine o'clock, so she stripped out of her clothes and put on her sleep shorts and long t-shirt. Maybe she would curl up in bed and read on her phone for a while.

When someone tapped on her door she figured it was Alyssa wanting to see her graduation pictures. She wasn't in the mood, so she would tell her they could look at them tomorrow. But when she opened the door it wasn't Alyssa at all, it was Adam, freshly shaved and showered, his hair still damp. He had on jeans and a T-shirt but his feet were bare.

"Oh, it's you." She stepped back so he could come in the door.

He raised an eyebrow. "Were you expecting someone else?"

"I wasn't expecting you." She shrugged.

He frowned. "Oh. Sorry I thought you wanted to... um... never mind." He turned to walk out the door.

"No. Wait." She grabbed his arm. He turned back to her, so she let go, even though she didn't really want to, it was a nice strong arm. "That's not what I meant. When you dropped off my stuff and then just left—I thought you'd changed your mind."

He shook his head and stepped closer. "No. I just didn't want to scratch you all up with my beard and figured I could use a shower."

"Oh. Well good. I guess. Very considerate of you... Um... I didn't shower. Or shave."

He looked her up and down slowly. Making her whole body tingle. "I doubt any hair you have—anywhere—will leave me with whisker burn. And you look adorable in your sleep shirt and tiny shorts."

She jerked back and looked down. "Oh, I forgot I was wearing them." She was embarrassed and confused and didn't know what to do to end this awkward encounter. Or —preferably—move it forward.

He shifted from foot to foot. "So, are you still interested in what we talked about earlier, or do you want me to get the hell out of your room?"

She smiled shyly. "How about you give me a little demonstration of what you have in mind."

His eyes heated, he stepped up to her and took her by the elbows pulling her in close. "I can do that."

Thank God.

~

ADAM LOWERED HIS HEAD SLOWLY, giving her time to get used to the idea, or run away if she wanted to. She didn't run away, she lifted her face up to him, speeding up the process. He took that as a good sign, so he placed his lips on hers, softly, reverently. Brushing his mouth back and forth over hers gently, forcing himself to go slow, when what he wanted to do was plunder.

He was still holding her by her elbows, but he felt her hands tracing a path up his back, so he let go of her elbows and wrapped his arms around her. She moved in closer, cementing her willowy body to his. Touching everywhere from knee to shoulder, they were nearly the same height, so she must be standing on her toes to bring them closer into alignment.

She pressed her mouth more firmly to his, so he obliged her with a firmer kiss. When her mouth opened he swept his tongue into the hot wet cavern, tasting a mintyness that was probably from toothpaste. But there was a taste—hovering below the mint—that was all her, and it was delicious. She moaned into his mouth and he tangled his hands in her hair, positioning her head to take the kiss further, deeper, into the heat.

Her hands found their way under his shirt in the back, they were strong and warm. He'd noticed her long slender fingers before, when she was taking photographs, but under his shirt they felt magnificent. His skin was on fire, sending shoots of lust south, making him harder by the second.

She rubbed up against him making his cock leap in enthusiasm. He pulled back from her hot hungry mouth, so he could breathe for just a moment.

Sucking in air, she looked up at him. "Yes."

Confused, he said, "Yes?"

She nodded. "Yes, I'm very much interested in what we talked about earlier. Did you bring protection?"

Fire shot through him, he wasn't sure he could speak. He nodded. "Of course. I'm the rules following, always prepared, first born." He gave her a crooked smile.

"Excellent, because I'm the rules following, only child."

She slid her hands back under his shirt pulling it up as she went. He obliged her by yanking it off and dropping it to the floor. Her eyes lit up as she looked him over and he was glad she liked what she saw.

"Nice," she cooed as her fingers started exploring.

He decided what was good for the goose was good for the gander, so he let his hands start roaming over the top of her T-shirt. She was petite, so it didn't look like she had a lot of curves, but that's not at all what it felt like to his seeking hands. She had a nice ass that filled his hands very well as he pulled her hips back to his.

She pinched his nipples which made his cock twitch. He bit down on her neck gently and then moved his hands up her sides until they found her breasts, which were also a very pleasant size. A perfect handful. Her nipples happily furled as he tweaked them through the T-shirt.

He growled out, "Mind if we lose the T-shirt?"

She shook her head. "Not at all, lose away."

He pulled the T-shirt over her head and tossed it aside. Taking his first good look at her his mouth watered, he wanted those lovely dusky rose nipples in his mouth. But that would be a lot easier on the bed, so he started walking her backwards. When her legs bumped against the mattress he followed her down.

Before moving down to her chest, he kissed her hard and long until she was gasping for breath. Then he started kissing and licking his way over to her ear which made her shudder. So, he lingered there another moment before continuing down her neck. He nipped at the shoulder and kissed away the sting, before moving to the soft center of her throat. Delving his tongue into the hollow, then kissing straight down her chest, until his face rested between her pert breasts. A very tempting place to stay, but those nipples were calling his name.

He wrapped one hand around one breast and took his lips over to the other one, pulling the tight nipple into his mouth. Her hips bucked off the bed as he suckled her, flicking his tongue over the turgid peak. Biting down gently she bucked again and he smiled against her breast, she seemed to like that. He worried that nipple a bit more before moving to the other one and giving it the same attention.

She was squirming under him. "Adam."

"Right here, lovely lady." He left her beautiful breasts to continue kissing his way lower. When he got to her sleep shorts he started dragging them off, and she lifted her hips to help. He pulled them off and noticed they were exceedingly wet, which made his cock twitch. But he planned to taste her, before he let the beast out.

He parted her legs and kissed up the inside of one, starting from her toes. When he got near her blazing hot center he stopped and went back down those magnificently long legs to start the process over on the second one. This time when he returned back to the apex he didn't hesitate but kissed her at her most sensitive spot. Then he separated those folds and feasted, while she thrashed on the bed.

~

RACHEL WAS sure she was going to die any moment or explode or maybe both. The man was killing her with wave after wave of pleasure. Her skin was on fire, she couldn't contain the sparks shooting through her whole body, from fingers and toes, to deep within her womb.

Then she did explode, light shooting from every corner of her being, sending her atoms into a cloud of shimmering brilliance.

She was certain her body could not recover and reconvene back into a solid form. She would have to live her life as a shimmering cloud. But as she lay there gasping for breath, her body did coalesce, and she became whole again.

Just in time to see Adam drop his jeans and roll on a condom. The man was magnificent and her body pulsed with wanting.

He looked at her and lifted an eyebrow in question.

She managed a nod. "Yes, please."

He grinned and came down on top of her, filling her with one long stroke. Her channel expanded making room for him, welcoming him into her body. It was glorious. She gripped his ass and pulled him in tighter, tilting her pelvis so he went deeper. As deep as he could go. She felt full. Complete. He pulled out and began long steady thrusts that caused her to start climbing that hill of pleasure a second time.

He loved her, over and over until her body was ready to explode again.

He growled in her ear. "Come for me."

And she did, her sex contracting around him and dragging him to completion with her, she milked him of every last drop. He collapsed on top of her pressing her into the mattress as he fought for breath. It was divine. She could happily stay like this for a week. If she didn't need to breathe that is, the man was heavy. Divine, but heavy.

He stirred and rolled them both to their sides. Removing the condom in the process and dropping it into the trash can next to the bed.

His sleepy eyes looked into hers and she smiled. He sighed and rested.

As he slept she wondered where this left them. Had they turned a corner? Or scratched an itch? She wasn't quite sure which she preferred.

CHAPTER 18

Adam woke up with a warm sexy woman wrapped around him, which felt really nice, but his brain was screaming at him. What in the hell had he just done? Had sex with a woman, nine years younger than he was, that's what. After all his self-righteous, judgmental pontificating toward Beau about being seven years older than Alyssa, he'd just done the same damn thing with an even wider gap in age.

He'd loved every minute of it. Even though he'd had to silence his thoughts. But once the deed was accomplished his convictions had roared back with a vengeance. So how to move forward? That was the real question. Pretend it didn't happen? Act like it was a one-time phenomenon? Enjoy her while she was here? A permanent relationship was not in the cards. He was still too old for her. He needed a mature woman by his side.

Maybe he could take his cues from her. Or maybe he should run like hell.

"Having second thoughts?" she asked.

Damn she'd caught him. Had he tensed up? "Not exactly. Just trying to figure out the next step."

She nodded, and her hair tickled his chest. "I was wondering the same thing, but it was too comfortable here with you to move. So, I decided not to think about it."

He sighed. "That is certainly one of the options. Maybe not the best one in the long run, but certainly appealing at the moment."

"We've got options. We can look at it as an itch scratched, one time, no harm no foul."

The easiest idea by far but for some reason he didn't really feel like the itch had been scratched. In fact, the idea kind of ticked him off.

She continued, "We can enjoy the time I'm here, in bed at the end of the day."

That sounded a little better, he would enjoy her. But was it courting disaster? Continuing a sexual relationship. And could he get his conscience to shut the hell up for that?

"We can play it by ear, on a day to day basis. Not crossing it off the list, but not making it a given either." He felt her shrug.

An interesting idea, but then how would they determine when they came together.

"We could develop some kind of code for it."

Shit, was she reading his mind?

"Like that old song, *Knock Three Times*."

A laugh burst forth. "That song from the seventies? How do you even know about that? You weren't even born yet. Hell, I wasn't born yet. For that matter my parents would have just been babies."

She giggled. "My grandmother loved *Tony Orlando and Dawn*. She played it often and we would dance to it. It's one of my favorite memories of her."

"A fun memory. Is she gone now?"

"About a year ago. I miss her a lot." Her breath caught, and he wished he hadn't asked.

He rubbed her back trying to ease the pain he was certain she was feeling. "I'm sorry."

She sniffed. "Changing the subject." Then she reached up and knocked three times on his headboard.

He wasn't about to disappoint a lady trying to reign in her sadness, so he let his hands roam her body, looking for ways to arouse her. He kissed the top of her head then her nose and settled on her mouth. He gave her long drugging kisses while his fingers lightly skimmed over her perfect body. Teasing, tickling, arousing every inch.

When he had her squirming, she reached down and took hold of his cock and ran her fingers up and down it until his eyes crossed.

He groaned. "Stop, or we won't be able to continue."

She grinned at him and reached for another condom he'd brought in with him and put on the night stand. She used her teeth to tear the package open and then rolled it on him. He gritted his teeth against the pleasure. When it was fully on, he slid between her legs and filled her.

She sighed in pleasure and he held still, loving the wet heat that surrounded him. After a few moments she wrapped her legs around his hips and he took that as the sign to start moving. They moved together in natural harmony that he'd never experienced before with a woman. For some strange reason their bodies seemed to be in sync with each other.

The pleasure built as he rocked into her again and again. Until he felt her body start to gather, so he sped up the friction to urge her on. She came hard, scratching his back in the process. He didn't mind, in fact, the slight pain carried him into an explosive orgasm that emptied him out.

When he gathered enough strength to move he rolled off her drawing her with him, so she ended on top. He didn't want to squish her. He was a big heavy guy and she needed to be able to breathe.

They stayed like that for a long time. Replete and relaxed. Eventually she moved off of him and he took that as his cue to leave. He gave her a long kiss. "I'm going back to my room now, sweet dreams, lovely lady."

She watched him dress and waved as he walked to the door. "Sweet dreams to you too, Adam."

He walked down the hall to his room and couldn't bring himself to regret his actions. It had been too perfect. Tomorrow it might haunt him, but tonight it felt excellent.

RACHEL WAS SATED AND BONELESS. When Adam got up to go back to his room she didn't feel the least bit disappointed. She just wanted to sleep, it had been a long day and she was tired. She waved goodbye to him and pulled the covers to her chin.

Before she could close her eyes, Alyssa burst in her door. Damn, she should have gotten out of bed when Adam left, and locked it.

Alyssa was standing just inside the door, still as a statue her mouth hanging open.

"If you're going to burst in my room the least you could do is shut the door."

Alyssa looked back at the door and then turned to Rachel, frowned and pushed the door closed and locked it.

Darn it. No sleeping for her, now. She sat up keeping the sheet over her. "Hand me my robe. It's on the closet door."

Alyssa looked at the closet door and back to Rachel still not saying a word.

This was getting old. "Alyssa, knock it off and hand me my damn robe. What the hell is wrong with you, anyway?"

Alyssa got the robe off the closet door hanger and handed it to her. "I'm just surprised. I saw Adam leave your room and was afraid he'd been in here being an ass. It never occurred to me you two were tearing up the sheets."

"My sheets are just fine, he was not being an ass, and we had two rounds of very excellent sex. Any other questions?" She lifted an eyebrow while holding the robe in one hand.

"You had sex with Adam? Twice?"

Rachel rolled her eyes at her friend. "Do I need to draw you a picture?"

Alyssa giggled. "Mr. High and Mighty had sex with a woman nine years younger, when he was giving Beau a hard time about me?" She laughed and clapped her hands. "That's awesome, I can't wait to tell Beau."

"Oh no, you don't. You might discuss everything with Beau, but I don't want my sex life broadcast about the house. Or Beau giving Adam a hard time."

"Well hell. I suppose you're right. It's not my place to say anything."

She put her arms through the robe and drew the front closed. "No, it's not, and it's not like we're going to get married, or anything. We are two single consenting adults, enjoying some intimacy."

"So, are you going to keep going at it?"

"I haven't decided."

Alyssa rubbed her hands gleefully. "Is that why he left? You kicked him out?"

"No, but I wasn't sad to see him leave, either. It's been a long day and I'm tired. I assume he is also. You know I'm not real fond of sharing a bed."

Alyssa laughed. "Yes, I am aware of that fact. You never did like to have me spend the night, unless I slept in the guest room."

Rachel shrugged. "I'm more comfortable alone."

"Okay. I see now that you didn't need me to rescue you, and you're right it's been a busy day. So, I'll get out of your hair and let you sleep. Alone. I wonder if you'll change your mind when you meet *the one*."

"Doubtful, thanks for coming to rescue me or cheer me up or whatever. Not to be rude but don't let the door hit you..."

Alyssa laughed and walked to the door. "You might want to lock this to keep people out... of your bed."

Rachel rolled her eyes and then did lock it once Alyssa was gone. Since she was up, she put on a nightgown, dropped her previous sleep clothes in the laundry basket, pulled her hair back in a tie, and climbed into bed. As she drifted off to sleep, she imagined Adam in the bed with her and found she didn't exactly hate the idea.

CHAPTER 19

Now that graduation was over, it was full steam ahead on the wedding plans. Rachel had no idea Alyssa could be such a drill sergeant. It was going to be a hurried planning period since the wedding was only two months away, so her friend's militancy was probably warranted. But Alyssa did not give her one moment to herself, and after a week she wanted a few minutes down time, and maybe some time with Adam again. She was beginning to think that wasn't going to happen any time soon. Alyssa had a time table that kept everyone hopping.

The engagement pictures and the wedding invitations arrived the same day, so Rachel, Emma, and Meg spent the next whole day stuffing envelopes. Alyssa insisted she address each invitation by hand because that showed the bride cared. Rachel thought it was a silly sentiment, but it was Alyssa getting the hand cramp not her, so she let her have her way.

Once the invitations were in the mail the four ladies decided to take a trip to Denver to find a dress for Alyssa. Tony was not happy about being left behind on a shopping expedition, but they all knew the little guy would be bored to tears within minutes. Candy and drug store shopping was one thing, wedding dress buying was another.

"Now Tony, uncle Cade and uncle Chase are going to take you out on the horses tomorrow, while us ladies go dress shopping." Emma dropped down to her knees and took him by the shoulders. "And then you and your uncles are going to do some fishing. Your papa is going to fry up those fish you catch."

Tony nodded and looked over at Travis. "Papa cooks fish real good."

"Yes, he does, and then you can play with all your uncles until bed time."

"Okay, Mama. Will you be home to tuck me in and kiss me g'night?"

"Probably not, but maybe you can have your uncles read you a book or two. And when I get home I'll come in and kiss you then. Deal?"

Tony nodded. "Deal." Rachel didn't think Tony was totally convinced but he was being brave.

Emma's smile was a little wobbly. "If you're really good for your uncles, I'll bring you back something special from Denver."

"I'll be good, Mama."

"I know you will, Tony. Now let's go on up and pick out your fishing clothes for tomorrow. Say goodnight to everyone."

Tony ran around the room giving everyone a goodnight hug. It was so darn cute Rachel had to smile. He even gave her a hug, which kind of surprised her, she wasn't very good with little kids, so hadn't expected one. But it melted her heart a little when he didn't exclude her.

Rachel stood. "I'm going to go get my cameras ready for the big day tomorrow, wedding dress shopping must be well documented." When she got to the door she turned and caught Adam's eye, then asked Alyssa what time they were leaving as she quietly knocked three times on the door frame, wondering if Adam was paying attention and would pick up on her action.

Out of the corner of her eye she saw him stiffen. When Alyssa reiterated the time, she glanced around the room and saw that Adam was looking at her intently. She gave a tiny nod and then bade the room goodnight.

She grinned as she walked to her room, wondering how long it would take him to follow.

ADAM COULD NOT BELIEVE the woman had just propositioned him in front of his entire family. They didn't realize what she was doing, of course. It had looked like a nervous action. His body had known and had leapt to attention. Which was going to make it damn difficult to gracefully leave the room any time soon.

She was probably laughing her ass off at leaving him this way. He might have to give her a swat for that, not mean of course, but just enough to sting a bit. Thinking about that idea made his condition worse. He needed to think of something else, anything else. Why in the hell couldn't he get his mind to focus? Because it already was focused on the woman currently sashaying her way to her room.

He'd had an idea for something to do with Tony, while Emma had been trying to convince him he would have fun staying home with them. What was it? It was a good idea and he couldn't remember it now to save him.

Finally, his brain regained a little blood and he remembered. "I was thinking when we put Tony to bed tomorrow, we should build a tent over his bed so it's like he's camping."

His brothers turned toward him with stunned expressions and he wondered if he'd said something else, like what he wanted to do with Rachel.

Chase broke the staring first. "That's a damn good idea, Adam. I was a little worried about bed time. But if we rig him up a tent and have him climb into that while we read him stories, that might just work."

Adam let out the breath he was holding, glad his mouth had said what he wanted to say instead of what he was thinking about.

Meg nodded. "I've got some old sheets you can use. You could use some thumb tacks in the ceiling or maybe get a couple of pieces of wood to tack the sheets on, to make tent posts."

Chad nodded. "And some twine to tie it all to the bed."

Adam groaned inwardly, he did not want to think about tying anything to a bed. Not with the state his body was in. But he'd diverted their attention and maybe he could make his getaway.

His dad said, "We could make the whole day kind of a camping theme. We could build a little campfire and roast the fish over that. Providing you catch anything." He grinned at the twins.

Chase rolled his eyes. "Of course, we will."

His mother smiled. "You could use some old pie tins and pretend they are old fashioned tin plates. Maybe heat up a can of beans with your fish. Roast some marshmallows and make s'mores."

Adam stood, his body finally beginning to calm down. "Well I'm glad you like my idea. I've got a couple of things I need to do tonight. See you all in the morning." They just barely acknowledged his leaving, they were so caught up in plans for entertaining Tony tomorrow. He rubbed his chin and decided he better shave before he went to visit Rachel, he didn't want to chafe her skin. She might be trying on dresses tomorrow and he didn't want to leave any evidence.

After a quick shave and tooth brushing he grabbed some condoms and walked down the hall to Rachel's door. He knocked three times thinking that would make her smile.

When she opened her door he about swallowed his tongue. She was smiling all right, but it was a smile of seduction, and her attire about brought him to his knees. She had on the skimpiest pajamas he'd ever seen. A short little flirty top hat hit her at the waist with matching, barely there panties, leaving a strip of skin between the two pieces.

"Took you long enough." She said and then turned her back on him and walked across the floor. He managed to get into the room and shut the door but that was about all the movement he had in him. He was pretty much frozen watching the amazingly sexy woman prance around in almost nothing.

She looked over her shoulder with a wicked grin. "Are you going to stand there all-night drooling?"

Was he drooling? It was entirely possible. He felt shell shocked. He needed to get it together before she rescinded her invitation. "Maybe. You look so amazing, I'm frozen."

"Well stop being frozen and get your butt over here. This outfit is not exactly warm and if you aren't going to help heat me up I'll have to put on a robe. A big floor length robe, of heavy terrycloth."

He shuddered at the thought of her covering up all that lovely skin. That would be a shame of the highest order. He looked her up and down one more time and then strode across the room and took her in his arms. "No need to do anything drastic. I'm more than happy to warm you up."

He rubbed his hands on her arms that did feel a little chilly. "You weren't joking, you're cold."

"I was waiting forever." She pouted.

"It's partially your fault it took so long. Knocking on that door frame got my whole body's attention. I had to wait until it calmed down and I could distract my family, before I could get up and walk out of the room." He kissed her neck and felt her shiver, he hoped it wasn't from the cold.

She giggled. "That is one advantage to being a female, our arousal is not so noticeable."

He leaned back and grinned at her. "Not until you get up close and personal. Then it's more obvious." Reaching down he squeezed her ass, pulling her in closer.

"You have too many clothes on, mister. Some of that nice hot skin would warm me right up. In more ways than one."

"I can fix that," he growled out. Then he whipped off his shirt and dropped it to the floor. Rachel purred and ran her hands over his chest. He unbuckled his belt and unzipped, to let his jeans fall down. It also freed his erection from the tight bind it had been subject to. Rachel brushed up against him and he groaned at the contact.

She brushed him again. "We could take advantage of the nice soft bed over there, with blankets to hold in all the heat."

Adam noticed she was still chilled, so he hoisted her up over his shoulder to carry her the two steps to the bed. "Your wish is my command." He pulled the blankets and quilt back, then dropped her on the bed so she bounced.

She laughed, and he slid in next to her, pulling the blankets back up over them. They might get too hot in a few minutes, but he needed to warm her up quickly. He didn't want her catching a chill because she was trying to be sexy for him.

He covered her mouth with his and held her close to share his body heat. She wasn't quite shivering but a few more minutes and she would have been. He kissed her long and slow and rubbed his large hands over her arms slowly to bring some warmth back into her skin. She squirmed to get closer and he leaned over, so his body was half on top of hers.

When she finally started to warm up and relax he ran a hand up under her short pajama top until he found her breast. He squeezed it gently and ran a thumb over her nipple. It tightened under his touch. She wrapped one leg around him and pushed her hot center on his leg.

He used all his previously learned knowledge of her body to arouse. Bringing her higher and higher until she was quaking under his hands and mouth.

She panted and pushed at him. "Adam, now. I want you inside."

He was beyond ready, his body screaming for more. He pushed the blankets off along with his shorts. While he rolled on a condom she flung her pajamas across the room and kicked the blankets away. Apparently, she was finally warm. He crawled on the bed and in between her legs, she wrapped around him like cellophane and he pushed into her warm wet channel.

"Perfect," she said on a sigh.

They spent most of the night wrapped in each other's arms. Sleeping and then waking to start the passion up again. He knew he was going to be tired tomorrow, but he didn't care. When it was getting close to dawn he quietly left her sleeping and went back to his room. She was an amazing lover, so giving and responsive. His previous experiences paled in comparison.

CHAPTER 20

The entire car was silent and sullen. They had just spent the entire day going from one bridal boutique to the next and they'd found nothing. Well nothing in the form of a dress anyway. They'd picked up random things in the boutiques, a veil, a ring bearer pillow, a flower girl basket—even though they didn't have a flower girl—fancy Champagne flutes, and a cake cutting set. But not the one thing they'd come to Denver for—the wedding dress.

They'd had no luck whatsoever. The dresses were either something Alyssa couldn't bear to wear, or they hadn't fit right and would need too many alterations to have it ready in time. She had wide shoulders and small breasts and she was too short for anything readymade. There were a couple she liked that could be made for her, but it was a six-month process.

Rachel could tell Alyssa was close to tears as she drove her Equinox down I-70 west. Her shoulders were tense, and her mouth was clamped into a line of frustration, her hands tense on the steering wheel. She had to think of something to give Alyssa hope.

Suddenly an idea formed. "Alyssa, what about having Barbara make you one?"

Alyssa's voice was rough with unshed tears. "I thought about that, but it takes Barbara forever to make dresses. Remember our prom formals, we tried them on a dozen times and it took her months. And those weren't nearly as complicated as a wedding dress."

"But maybe you should ask. She might have some ideas."

Alyssa shook her head. "I don't think—"

The car phone cut Alyssa off mid-sentence. She pushed the talk button. "This is Alyssa."

"Alyssa, this is Barbara Clarkson."

"Hi Barbara, we were just talking about you."

Rachel spoke up. "Hi Barbara, this is Rachel, we're in the car driving back from Denver."

Barbara said, "Hi Rachel, what were you girls doing in Denver?"

"Looking for a wedding dress."

Barbara sniffed. "Did you find one?"

Alyssa sighed. "No, we did not."

"Well good, because you are totally going to hurt my feelings if you don't let me make you one." Barbara said sharply.

"But the wedding is in two months, it's not enough time."

"Alyssa Jefferson, you and your big day are more important than any other client I have. Besides my staff can take care of the other clients while I focus on you. How many bridesmaids are you having?"

"Just Rachel and Beau's sister Emma, who's also in the car."

"Perfect. I'll do their dresses, too."

Alyssa looked at Rachel and she shrugged. "But what about fittings and stuff?"

"I have an invitation in my hand for a bridal shower in a month. I assume you're coming to it."

"Yes."

"That will work perfectly. I'll send you some sketches, you pick the one you like best and I'll have them ready for the first fitting before the shower and a second fitting after the bachelorette party. Then we'll do the final fitting and adjustments the week before the wedding. Chris and I are coming out early."

Alyssa frowned. "You and Chris are driving out for the wedding?"

"Well, of course we are."

"But what about your businesses?" Alyssa asked, and Rachel had to admit she wondered about it too. Barbara had a thriving online wedding dress design business and she also was a partner in a wedding and costume boutique in town. Chris was the spearhead of a large amusement park, based on a video game one of the residents had designed in high school and sold to a tech company in Seattle.

"That's the beauty of owning your own. Chris and I are the bosses and can leave when we like. I've already made reservations at the Singing River Ranch. The woman assured me we could have a cabin that has enough room for my sewing machine and plenty of room for Jill to play."

Alyssa's breath caught, and Rachel looked at her to see an expression of delight. "Barbara, do you think Jill would be able to be in the wedding, as a flower girl?"

"Oh..." There was a shuffling sound and Rachel wondered what had happened.

"Barbara?" Alyssa said

"Alyssa? This is Chris. Barbara needs a moment."

Rachel said, "Hi Chris, this is Rachel. Does Barbara's needing a moment mean what I think it does?"

Rachel was certain she could hear the man's chest puff out. "Yes, Rachel. Little Jill is going to have a baby brother before the end of the year."

Rachel and Alyssa grinned at each other when they heard Barbara say, "Chris you are such a blabber-mouth, now give me my phone. Alyssa, we would be honored to have Jill be your flower girl. I'll make her a dress to match your bridesmaids'."

"Oh goody." A thrilled smile covered Alyssa's face.

"I'll need your colors and Emma's measurements. You and Rachel are still relatively the same size you were in high school, aren't you?"

Rachel nodded, and Alyssa answered, "Yes, we haven't changed much."

"Good. Then I have your measurements from your prom dresses. I'll sketch up some ideas and email you," Barbara said decisively.

"Don't you want to ask me what I like?" Alyssa asked.

"Alyssa, I've known you since you were a toddler. I'm fairly certain I can send you some ideas to start with, you can fine tune whichever one you like best." Rachel had to admit if anyone knew what Alyssa would like it would be Barbara, when it came to clothing the woman was hawk-eyed.

Alyssa said, "Awesome, thanks, Barbara."

"You're welcome, I'm just glad you didn't find some nasty dress in Denver. Honestly, I don't know why you even looked. Send me colors and measurements. Oh, and Emma will need to come with you to the bridal shower, so she can be fitted too."

Emma said, "Hi Barbara, this is Emma. I will be happy to come."

"Good, I need to go now. I'll email you, Alyssa."

Before they could say goodbye, the car phone signaled the call was over.

Meg laughed. "That woman is a force to be reckoned with. How did you know she was pregnant, Rachel?"

Rachel looked into the back seat and gave Meg a grin.

"Barbara gets very emotional when she's pregnant and bursts into tears at the slightest provocation. She runs off to the bathroom and then comes out a few minutes later and acts like nothing happened. When she's not pregnant she is never emotional. The first time she got pregnant everyone thought she'd gone crazy, but as soon as little Jill was born Barbara settled right down to her normal self."

Meg laughed. "Pregnancy does affect each person differently."

"Well at least our wedding dress dilemma is taken care of," Emma said cheerily.

Alyssa sighed, and Rachel was thankful to see a wide smile on Alyssa's face as she said, "Thank God for that. Barbara does such an excellent job on her dresses, it will be perfect."

Emma asked, "How old is Jill?"

Alyssa shrugged and glanced at Rachel. "Four, about the same age as Tony actually. They will be adorable together."

The rest of the drive back was happy and they all chattered about the wedding and who all might be driving in from Washington. Alyssa didn't think many would be joining them. Rachel on the other hand, would be surprised if there was anyone left in Chedwick, Washington the weekend of the wedding. She suspected some of them would fly into Denver if they didn't have the four days to spend driving back and forth.

Adam collapsed into an overstuffed chair in the living room as his father and brothers did the same. Tony had run all six of them ragged. He honestly did not know how Emma did it, day after day. There'd been six of them and they were exhausted. Emma took care of him all day every day, attended night classes online in the evenings and did bookkeeping on the weekends while his mom watched Tony.

The six of them had been in charge of the boy for twelve hours and could barely move. He hoped like hell that the women had found dresses, so they would not have to go shopping and leave the boy with them for the whole day again. An hour or two here and there was fine, but twelve hours was killer. He had a whole new respect for his sister. The woman was clearly made of stronger stuff than he was.

Beau shook his head. “I don’t know how Emma does it.”

Chase opened his eyes. “Right? I was thinking the same thing.”

Dad rubbed the back of his neck and sat up. “You know, we can’t let on that the little guy tuckered us out this much, or we will never hear the end of it.”

He and all four of his brothers groaned at the truth of the statement.

“Coffee? Energy drinks? Sugar?” Cade said looking at each of them.

“Not coffee or energy drinks, caffeine lasts too long. Sugar is the best bet, it will give us some energy, but not enough we won’t be able to sleep,” Adam said.

Cade nodded. “True. Cookies or ice cream?”

Drew stood. “Both. I’ll dish up the ice cream. Cade, you get the cookies. The rest of you drag your butts to the kitchen.”

The ice cream and cookies did start to revive them and as they ate they laughed about the events of the day. Tony had been thrilled to be allowed to ride his own horse. Cade had led the gentle mare by the reins as Tony perched on top. He’d always only ridden with another adult, so he’d been in hog heaven, all alone. Chase had been on one side with their dad on the other so either one could catch him if something went wrong. But it hadn't, and Tony's grin was huge when they got to the river.

The fishing had been a hoot. Tony loved playing with the worms they'd dug up to use so they had resorted to using salmon eggs. Drew and Adam had brought along their fly fishing rods, so they would be certain to have some fish for dinner. Chase and Cade were so busy with Tony they didn't really have time to fish at all.

They stopped for a while and had a picnic lunch of peanut butter and jelly sandwiches, chips, apples and water. After lunch Tony did manage to catch one fish and as far as he was concerned he was the best fisherman ever. When he pulled the fish in, he'd gotten a little too close to the river and ended up wet from his knees down. Fortunately, that incident was toward the end of their fishing time, so they could get him home without being too cold. It was a warm day, but it was still in the mountains of Colorado and the water that fed the river was made up of snow melt, so it was icy cold.

When they got back to the ranch they made Tony take a bath. The water was practically black from the little guy digging in the dirt and playing with the worms. Then he took a short nap on the couch with Grandpa K, while the brothers put away all the fishing equipment, brushed down the horses, cleaned the fish and set up the camp fire. Travis made some corn bread and Grandpa K doctored up some pork and beans. They set up some logs to sit on by the fire and brought out the pie tins to use as plates.

When Tony got up from his nap he was raring to go. They played Cowboys and Indians around the campfire and eventually got around to cooking over the flames. Tony declared it was the best meal he'd ever eaten. Once they got some real food in him they let him roast marshmallows to make s'mores. He ended up just as dirty from the playing in the dirt, being near the fire, sticky marshmallows and gooey chocolate as he had from fishing, so he had to take a second bath and then they all went into his room to see his tent bed.

He was so excited he bounced all over the room. They finally got him calmed down enough to read him some stories.

He was almost asleep when he cried out, "But mommy can't kiss me if I'm in the tent, she won't be able to reach me when I'm asleep." His chin started to tremble and all six of them panicked not wanting him to start crying.

Grandpa K heard the commotion and came into the room to ask what was wrong. Tony explained with tears forming in his eyes.

Grandpa K calmly said, "We can fix that easy as pie, don't you worry one bit. Chase get a piece of paper and a marker. Drew get some scissors or a sharp knife. Chad, there's twine in the mud room, grab a couple feet of it. Adam there are safety pins in Meg's sewing kit. Beau read the boy another story while we fix up his tent."

When they all returned with their assigned items. Grandpa K said. "Chase, write *Mother kisses here*. Drew, cut two nice long slits in the tent right where Tony's pillow is to make a flap. We'll pin the sign above the flap and tie the twine to the bottom of it, so Emma can lift it easily in the dim light."

Tony had stopped listening to the story and was watching them work to fix his dilemma. When it was ready he went over to look at it. He pulled on the string and saw it lift the flap. When he saw his pillow right behind it he grinned and hugged Grandpa K. "You're the smartest Grandpa ever."

Grandpa K patted the boy on the back. He cleared his throat. "Now get on in your bed and we'll try it out to make sure it works."

Each one of them gave the boy a good night kiss through

the tent flap and he drifted off to sleep with a smile on his face. The men walked silently out of the room knowing they had dodged a bullet. Happy, but exhausted.

As they laughed about the day while eating ice cream and cookies they discussed how much to tell Emma and the other women. They certainly didn't want to tell them that the little guy had run them ragged. They weren't sure they wanted to mention him getting wet at the river or the fact that they'd had to give him two baths.

Adam was sure Rachel would get a kick out of the pictures they'd taken with their phones. Rachel? Why was he thinking about her? The pictures were of Tony, so Emma would love them. Actually, all four of the women would enjoy the pictures, but he wondered why his mind had gone straight to Rachel, bypassing his sister.

CHAPTER 21

Every day more RSVPs came in for the wedding, nearly all of them affirmative. Rachel thought Alyssa was going to have a breakdown. She on the other hand was not at all surprised, Alyssa was a favorite in their small town. If Rachel was getting married she didn't think nearly as many people would be driving for two days each way to attend. In fact, Rachel thought it was kind of silly for them to be getting married in Colorado, but she had to admit just as many people from Colorado were planning to attend.

Rachel was logging the responses while Alyssa opened the envelopes. After they finished with the mailed cards, they would check the online responses.

Alyssa gasped. "You are not going to believe it."

Of course, Rachel was going to believe it, since Alyssa had been saying that very same thing for the last twenty minutes. And every day before that when they went through the mail, and the bridal website.

"Who is it this time?"

"Mrs. Erickson."

Rachel raised her eyebrows. "Now that one is a surprise. She's gotta be in her eighties."

"Yeah, she retired from teaching the year we would have been in her class, and I think she was nearly seventy then. We were eight, so fourteen years ago, yep eighty at least."

"I hope the trip doesn't kill her, that would not be good." Rachel shivered.

"Oh, don't you worry about that, my friend, that woman can run circles around all of us."

Rachel nodded. "You do have a point. Do you know she joined the yoga class, and my mom said she put everyone to shame?"

Alyssa laughed. "I don't doubt that for one minute."

"Does it say how she's getting here?"

Alyssa scanned the return and then burst out with a loud guffaw. "It says her plus one is Greg Jones. So, I'm guessing he's bringing her, or escorting her if they fly."

"For all his bad to the bone exterior, he's really a nice guy."

"I don't see him as bad to the bone, more super intense. I think running the bar is what makes him appear bad, but he's also the assistant fire chief, so not really bad in any way." Alyssa pointed at her.

"I had a terrible crush on him when we were younger." Rachel admitted.

Alyssa rolled her eyes. "No. Really? Is that why we had to walk by his bar every day after school and just happened to go by the fire department on Saturdays when they practiced? I saw right through you, girlfriend."

Rachel shrugged as she felt her face heat. "It was my first real crush. I wonder why no woman has ever snatched him up."

"There's a lot of good-looking guys in our town still fighting the wedding ring."

Rachel nodded as she thought about it. "True, there's Greg, Terry, Kyle, even pastor Scott."

"Exactly. That's the last of the paper responses, let's check the website."

As Alyssa booted up her computer and logged into the website, Rachel thought about men avoiding commitment and wondered about the fact that all the Kipling men except Beau were still single with no girlfriends. Well, Cade kind of had a girlfriend. She didn't seem very nice and bossed him around a lot. Which surprised Rachel because he was such an easy going flirty guy. How did the nice ones always end up with the bitchy women?

She shrugged and then thought about she and Adam, they'd had sex a half dozen times, but they had no relationship outside the bedroom. Sometimes they would exchange greetings, but that was about all. He was still planning to help her take all the pictures for Beau's college presentation after all the wedding hub-bub had died down.

Alyssa whacked her on the arm. "You aren't listening to me. Are you mooning over Greg or Adam?"

Rachel frowned. "No. I am not mooning over anyone, just thinking about the pictures Beau asked me to take for his presentation."

Alyssa nodded smugly. "Uh huh, with Adam helping you find each animal."

Rachel rolled her eyes. "I'm listening now, let's get on with it."

"Fine. Amber and Jeremy Scott are coming. Seriously they are just going to have to shut down the town, there won't be anyone running the restaurants with your mom and Amber both coming. And Greg's bar and the amusement park, although Chris has a lot of staff running it, so maybe it can stay open. And the big hotel on the lake is run by the corporation so it has restaurants."

Rachel said, "Some people might be planning to fly in for the day and fly out at night. They can catch a flight out of Spokane or drive to Seattle. That would only be a day or two away from town."

"Oh look, Sandy is coming!" Alyssa crowed.

"That one is not a surprise, she was our baby sitter until she went to college. I imagine the rest of the Anderson's will come too."

"Yeah, you're right Sandy is accepting for her, Terry and Mayor, I mean, former Mayor Carol. I can't get used to someone else being the mayor even if it is Chief MacGregor or Mayor MacGregor… now that Nolan Thompson is police chief. What a tangle."

Rachel said smugly, "Not for those of us that didn't leave town right after the elections. We're all used to it."

"But she did not accept for Janet, Brett's probably going to be on the road and she's probably not allowed to go anywhere without him. Plus, Nolan and Kristen are not coming. Not a big surprise since someone has to stay and be the police chief and Kristen is not the most outgoing person on the planet. Although I've always liked her."

Rachel nodded. "Yeah she's been good to me with having my pictures in her art gallery. But I don't think she would be too thrilled about being in the middle of your ginormous wedding. She barely let Chris and Barbara attend her marriage to Nolan. Her own sister. No wedding shower, no reception. The woman is still pretty much a recluse even though she lives in town. But I'll bet she sends you some killer piece of jewelry as a wedding present."

Alyssa's eyes lit up. "Oh, do you think so? That would be awesome."

"Yep and if I know her, it will be here in time for the wedding and will go perfectly with the dress her sister is making for you."

Alyssa squealed. "Oh, you're probably right. I can't wait!"

"Can't wait for what?" Beau asked as he came into the room and kissed Alyssa on top of her head.

Alyssa jumped up and wrapped him in a hug. "It's a secret. For the wedding day."

"Sexy lingerie?" he asked hopefully.

"No silly, although I might be able to find something like that, too."

Rachel rolled her eyes. "I think the town ladies will have you covered for that at the shower."

ADAM CLEARED HIS THROAT. Why? Why had he followed Beau into where the women were working on the wedding stuff? He didn't need to hear about sexy lingerie, because that got him to thinking about Rachel draped in scraps of lace. And that was not a good idea because his body liked that image a lot. He ignored the thought and his reaction. He cleared his throat again, shifting his stance a bit to make himself more comfortable and less visible to the women.

"So, we came in here for a reason, ladies." He nudged Beau to get his mind back on track.

Beau shook his head, like he was coming out of a trance. "Right."

He shook his head again and looked at Adam. "But I can't remember what it was now, all my brain cells melted."

Adam folded his arms and glared at his brother.

Alyssa grinned, and Rachel rolled her eyes as they all looked expectantly at Beau.

Beau frowned as he looked back at them. Adam couldn't believe his brother, he'd been yammering all morning about his plans. Until Adam wanted to punch him in the mouth, to shut him the hell up. Rather than resorting to violence, he'd suggested taking the girls out on the horses to get their opinion, instead of guessing what it would be. Beau had liked that idea and both of them decided the girls could use a break from wedding planning.

Adam finally gave up and said, "We've got horses saddled—"

Beau interrupted, "Oh right. Can you tear yourselves away from wedding planning for a little while? I've got something I want to show you." He hopped from foot to foot like a little kid would.

Alyssa smiled. "Sure, we were just logging the RSVPs, but we're done now."

Beau grabbed Alyssa's hand and dragged her with him, toward the door. "Perfect."

Rachel looked at Adam. "Camera?"

"Oh yeah," he said.

She nodded. "Be right back." And dashed off toward her room. He thought that this was the first time he'd seen her outside of her room when it wasn't in her hand.

She hurried back, and they went to get boots and a light jacket—just in case. Beau and Alyssa were in the yard with a saddle bag of first aid supplies, bottles of water and apples. Adam decided that was a good idea, taking something to munch on.

"Smart to bring some fruit." He stuffed his water and apple into a saddle bag and tied the jacket to the saddle, as everyone else did the same.

Rachel swung onto her horse and looked down at her jeans. "Oh, maybe I should have changed, these are kind of worn out. I didn't plan to leave the house. They are my comfy staying at home jeans."

Adam shrugged. "A tear in the knee isn't going to matter,

we're staying on the property, so not a big deal. Other than you might get a sunburn." He gave her a lopsided grin.

She laughed, and the sound shimmered through him. He just loved her laugh, and she was so free with it. He was going to miss that laugh when she went back home or off to art school.

CHAPTER 22

Rachel was happy to be out in the sunshine. Colorado had the prettiest days. It was almost always sunny, the air was so fresh and clean, the sky so blue it almost hurt to look at it. It was still slightly cool out this morning, but it felt like it was going to be a warm day. They'd been so busy lately they hadn't had any time outside in days. But things were starting to come together and not a moment too soon.

They would be leaving for Chelan in a little over a week for the bridal shower and dress fittings. Tony was going with them and he could hardly wait for the road trip. The first few hours would be easy, but after that he might get bored. They'd all been thinking about ways to keep him entertained for two days in the car. A tablet loaded with movies and games would go a long way, but they needed some other alternatives, too.

Her musings came to a halt when Beau and Alyssa turned into the trees. She and Adam followed them on a path and stopped their horses in a pretty little clearing. She could hear the river but couldn't see it. Adam looked at her and mouthed *camera* so she quickly got it out of the bag.

Beau slid off his horse and the rest of them followed suit. He tied his horse to a nearby tree, so they did too. Then he walked a little further into the clearing.

Rachel started snapping pictures, assuming Adam knew what was going on.

"What is this?" Alyssa asked.

Beau looked at her and grinned. "My land to build a house on."

Alyssa screeched. "Really? Our own house?" She clapped her hands together and then frowned. "Not that I mind living with your parents... but it's so beautiful."

"I think so. Each of us have a location on the property to build our own house. This lot's big enough for a house, a garage and a small barn. Maybe a kitchen garden or flowers." Beau went over to Alyssa and took her hand. "I wanted you to see it, so we can decide how soon we want to start building, or at least designing what we want."

"Oh today, no yesterday! I'm so excited." She started chattering about ideas and walked around pointing. Beau laughed, clearly delighted with her enthusiasm.

Rachel continued to document her happiness, while wondering where Adam's house location was.

Adam walked up next to her. "Let's go over by the river and give them a few minutes privacy."

She nodded. "That's an excellent idea."

Beau and Alyssa were so caught up, she didn't even think they noticed her and Adam walk into the trees, on the other side of the clearing.

When they got to the river Rachel took some pictures of it. "So where is your land?"

He pointed. "See that speck of red down there on the other side of the river bend. It's behind that."

Rachel used her telephoto lens to zoom in on the speck of red and saw it was some kind of bench. "What is a bench doing way out here?"

"It's a swing. My grandmother loved that spot on the river, so Grandpa K built her a swing. When I was little I used to ride down here with her and sit on the swing and she would tell me stories. When she died a few years ago we put the cushions away, but we didn't let it rust. I think we all check on it to make sure it's sealed against the weather. Anyway, when we divvied up the land I picked that location."

Rachel had a lump in her throat and couldn't speak, so she took a couple of pictures to hide her emotions. When she could finally swallow she asked, "Is it close enough to walk to?"

"Yeah there's a path between the two, actually there's a path all along the river except when the beaver dams get in the way. Want to walk down?"

She looked back toward where Beau and Alyssa were, wondering if she should tell them they were going. But not wanting to interrupt.

"Don't worry about those two, if they remember we were with them, they can always text us."

"True. Yes, let's walk down there."

ADAM WANTED to show Rachel his land. He was proud of it and wanted to share it with her. He'd never shown anyone outside of the family his property. He'd thought a long time about what kind of house he wanted and where he planned to put it. But that's all the further it had gone, oh he had some sketches drawn up but nothing concrete. It seemed silly to go to all the work to build, just for himself. But the idea had become more appealing as his brother had talked about building a house for Alyssa. Maybe he wouldn't wait too long. He'd let Beau get his house built and then look into starting on his own. Although it might be easier and cheaper to do some of it in tandem, like running electricity. He'd have to look into things like that. All six of them were getting to be an age they might want to be moving out. It might be wise to run all the electricity and water at one time. He should talk to his dad about that.

Rachel interrupted his thoughts. "Have you or Beau thought about what you want to build?"

"I can't say what Beau has planned, but I have put some thought into mine."

"I would love to hear your ideas." She hurried on, "Just for fun, of course."

"Of course." But he didn't really like the sound of that. He liked that she was interested. "I've got some sketches back at the house. I'd be happy to hear your input. A woman has a different perspective than a man does."

"That would be fun."

They followed the path a little further and it turned to follow the river. There were trees in the way, as they went through a more densely forested area. When they came out of it, he drew back to watch her reaction.

She looked up and saw the swing, her face lit with joy and she gasped. "Oh, Adam this is so beautiful." She paused to take several pictures of the pretty spot. The swing sat in a small clearing close to the river, wildflowers grew all over the ground, columbine, black eyed Susan's, avalanche lilies, alpine buttercup. It was a profusion of color. And the swing sat in the middle of it with pine trees and aspen ringing the ground, the sunlight lighting the area.

After taking pictures, she hurried over and sat on the swing looking out at the river. He watched her face and saw her give a big sigh and smile serenely. He always felt pretty much the same way when he visited this land. It was pretty and peaceful. He went over and sat next to her on the swing. It wasn't terribly comfortable without the cushions, but the surroundings made up for that.

Rachel whispered, "This is amazing. I could sit here forever."

He nodded and took her hand. They sat there absorbing the peace, listening to the river rush past. He'd not sat on this swing with another person since his grandmother had died, but somehow this just felt right, sharing the space with Rachel.

CHAPTER 23

Rachel loved this little clearing and didn't want to move. The companionship she felt with Adam sitting next to her was something she'd never experienced before. She leaned her head on his shoulder and listened to the river.

The peace was shattered by his phone ringing. He answered with a terse, "What Beau?"

He listened. "On grandma's bench."

He nodded. "We'll meet you in my house clearing."

Hanging up the phone he turned to Rachel. "They're going to bring the horses down in a few minutes. Want to go see the rest?"

She really didn't want to move, but she smiled at him. "Sure, just a couple more pictures." She took pictures of the river from the bench and a few of the various wildflowers. She wanted to remember the peace she'd felt in this spot, pictures wouldn't do it justice, but they would help remind her.

Adam led the way down a different path that ran perpendicular to the river and away from it. They came out of the trees and went up a slight hill to a nice large clearing. "Oh, this is great. You can see all the way over to the national forest area, can't you?"

"Yes, I like the view."

She laughed. "Me, too." She took pictures of the clearing as he explained his ideas for building. Then she put on the telephoto lens and took pictures of the mountains in the distance. A small black object came into view and she zoomed in on it and gasped.

"What is it?" Adam asked.

"The drone. I'm going to try to follow its movements with my camera." She started taking pictures as it moved.

"It's heading toward the national forest I think." She kept her lens zoomed in enough to follow it but far enough out to be able to see it's trajectory.

"Yes, it's going further away. I hope I don't lose it in the trees. No, it's going higher to avoid them."

Beau and Alyssa rode up, but she didn't take her eyes off the drone.

"Rachel has the drone in her sights and she's following its path," Adam said.

Beau replied, "Good maybe she can see where it goes. We could follow it on the horses."

"Oh! It's heading up that mountain. The flat one." Rachel cried out.

Adam groaned. "The plateau? Well, hell, that makes sense. I saw a tent up there a couple of weeks ago. I thought it was kind of an odd place to camp but didn't think that much about it."

Rachel couldn't see the drone any longer, it had either landed or gone over the other side of the mountain. She put her camera down. "I don't see it anymore."

Alyssa said, "Let's go check it out."

Adam shook his head. "I don't think that's such a good idea, I don't think you girls should go."

"Phffft." Alyssa said as she reigned her horse around. "I'm not worried. I'm going."

Beau shrugged.

Adam frowned, clearly not on board with the idea of them going to check it out. "But what if the guy is armed? Or dangerous."

Alyssa said, "We can be quiet and observe the camp from a distance with Rachel's camera and if he looks armed and dangerous we can call the cops to come deal with him."

Beau nodded. "We could probably do that, we know that mountain pretty well from the days we used to camp—or more recently—drink up there."

Adam rubbed his chin. "We could come in from the north, the tent I saw faced south and was on the west side close to where you can see the ranch. Okay let's give it a try, but if it looks dangerous we stop and head straight back to the ranch. We can call Drew."

Beau nodded. "Sounds like a plan."

Rachel had been listening to this exchange as she looked through the pictures she'd taken of the drone. "I think it has cameras on it."

Adam frowned. "Let me see."

She zoomed into the area she thought held the cameras and showed it to Adam who passed it to Beau and finally Alyssa. Waiting to see if they agreed with her and wondering why someone would mount cameras on a drone. Flying over the ranch and taking pictures seemed like a kind of strange activity.

Adam nodded. "I think you're right. That seems kind of odd."

Rachel looked at him. "That's what I thought, too."

"Come on let's go investigate," Alyssa said.

Everyone nodded and mounted their horses.

~

ADAM WASN'T sure this was the wisest course of action, but he'd been out voted. They rode out into the clearing and headed north, even though the most direct route would have been straight west. But if the person was on the plateau he or she would be able to see them coming and hide. So, by going north they could go into the trees where they couldn't be seen from the plateau, because it had trees of its own on the north side.

He wondered if he should call his brother or the police station and let them know what they were doing. But decided if it was just one person which is what the camping spot had indicated, they should be fine. And if the person looked armed or dangerous, they didn't have to confront him.

They raced across the pasture both the humans and the horses enjoying the run. It didn't take them long to get far enough north to enter the trees.

Adam said, "We can go in here and take the horses up for a bit. When we get close we'll tie them up and go in on foot."

Beau nodded. "I agree with that plan."

Rachel suggested, "We could just act like we're on a hike and see if he'll chat with us."

"Yeah, that way it won't get him all upset. Well as long as he doesn't look crazy or something. If that's the case we book it down the mountain and call the cops," Alyssa said.

Adam agreed, "Sounds like a plan." They all nodded their agreement.

They followed a path up the mountain until they knew they were getting close, so they tied off the horses next to a tiny stream where there was some grass growing and went the rest of the way on foot.

When they reached the top of the plateau they went quietly through the trees until they could see the camping area. There was a single man sitting on a rock holding the drone. It looked like he might be looking at the cameras strapped to the thing. There was nothing else near him. No firearms to be seen. He was dressed in jeans, a plaid shirt and hiking boots. He wasn't a big guy, in fact he looked kind of nerdy.

Adam motioned that he was going to go around to the side, so they could come in from two angles. Beau nodded. Rachel followed him, and he decided that was a good idea to go in as two pairs.

When he got in position he waved at Beau, took Rachel's hand and they walked into the clearing as if they were on a hike. Alyssa and Beau did the same. The man was so busy looking at his drone's camera that he didn't notice them until they were right on top of him.

Adam said, "Hello, what'cha got there, friend?"

The man startled and looked up. Adam saw him glance down at an old paper. He kind of turned his body as if to shield it.

Adam thought the paper looked vaguely familiar but didn't want to stare at it and make the guy more uncomfortable, so he plastered a smile on his face. "I'm Adam Kipling, this is my girlfriend, Rachel. Those two are my brother Beau and his fiancé Alyssa. And you are?"

Adam stood there waiting to see what the guy was going to do. It took him a couple of minutes before he finally said, "I'm Pete, just doing some camping in the national forest. Nothing wrong with that."

Adam nodded. "Nope, not at all. We used to camp up here all the time when we were kids and thought we were going on a grand adventure. Had some keggers up here, a time or two as we got older. Last one was about five years ago when a buddy was getting ready to join the pro-rodeo circuit. Good times."

As Adam blabbed on he saw the guy relax a bit. Adam noticed Beau had shifted a little while Adam kept the guy's attention on him. From where he was now standing Adam thought Beau might be able to get a better look at the paper the guy was hiding.

Adam continued to distract the guy. "Have you done any camping further into the forest? There are some great trails and much prettier scenery to the north a bit. Here you can't see much besides our ranch."

"Not yet, I'll probably venture in further, trying out some new equipment first."

Adam nodded. "Like that drone, I suspect. Seen it a time or two on the ranch. About beaned me and my horse one time." He chuckled. "Scared the living daylights out of my horse. Nearly ended up walking back, but the girls came and rescued me."

"Oh, uh, sorry about that. Darn thing has a mind of its own sometimes and gets away from me."

What a pile of horse shit, the guy was spewing, but Adam plastered a grin on his face. "Yes, sir. I imagine it takes some skill to learn to fly one. I've not played with one myself. Always looked like fun though."

Pete said, "I'm getting the hang of it now."

Suddenly a grin lit up Beau's face. He looked like he might bust a gut, he was trying so hard not to laugh.

He reached down and picked up the paper. "Hey man, where in the hell did you get a copy of this birthday party treasure map? I haven't seen one in years."

"Give me that, it's mine." Beau handed it right over to him, still grinning. "What do you mean birthday party?"

Beau didn't answer him directly. "Adam, this guy has a copy of the treasure map we put together for the twins when they were ten, haven't seen a copy in a good fifteen years."

"No, I don't. This is much too old to be only fifteen years old."

Adam stepped closer and peered at the paper. "Sure does look like the one we made." He turned to Pete. "We researched how to make paper look old, worked on it about a month. The twins wanted an Indiana Jones birthday, so we came up with the idea of a treasure map and wanted it to look realistic."

"I don't believe you," Pete said. "You're trying to trick me."

"Nope, no need to do that. Have you figured out what the markings on the back are." Adam was grinning now, too.

Pete shook his head.

Adam put his hand out. "Mind if I show you? I'll give it right back."

Curiosity won out over mistrust and the man handed the paper to Adam. He quickly folded it in a few places and handed the finished product back to Pete.

Pete looked at it. "Well hell. It's a frigging birthday cake with a number ten on the top and the initials CC."

Beau nodded. "The twins Chase and Cade were ten years old. The treasure was cake and ice cream and their presents, and a small chest of gold foil covered chocolate coins for each of them. That looks like the treasure chests on the front of the map. The folded part is a nod to our mother's favorite romance movie."

Pete's face had turned red. "Do you mean to tell me, I've been on this damn table mountain for three months, sending my drone all over your land looking for the exact spot this map indicates and it was for a children's party? God damn it all to hell."

Adam nodded and waved his hand toward their ranch.

"Afraid so, my friend. No real treasure is on that land unless you count the cows or the hay."

Beau interjected, "There are some stories of lost gold or gold mines to the north or west about 50 miles, or Gilpin county has its fair share, but nothing around here. No train robberies, no gold mines, nothing exciting. Believe me with five boys in the family we tried to find any hint of something to search for and came up with nothing. Not even an old arrow tip."

Pete dropped the treasure map to the ground and started packing up his gear. Beau looked at Adam and lifted an eyebrow. Adam gave him a slight head shake; the guy had already been punished enough—in his opinion—no need to press charges.

Beau nodded. "Want some help packing up?"

"No thanks. I'm too pissed to be good company."

Beau shrugged. "I can understand that, well good luck on your next attempt."

Adam asked, "Do you mind if we take the map back? The twins might get a kick out of seeing it again."

"Nope, feel free." Pete grumbled between clenched teeth.

Adam swooped it up, and they all turned to leave, hiding their smiles so it didn't piss the guy off even more. When they got back to the horses they laughed and talked about it as they rode back to the house. Dinner that night was uproarious as they told the story and passed the *treasure map* around.

Adam was relieved the mystery was solved and no one had gotten hurt. Even though the guy was trying to steal from them, he still found himself feeling a little sorry for him. He could imagine the anticipation of finding a big treasure, working for weeks toward that goal, and then finding out it was a fake.

CHAPTER 24

Adam was feeling restless. He didn't want to admit it, but the reason for his mood was that the women would be returning today. They'd been gone a week and he was looking forward to their return. He'd been shocked at how much he'd missed seeing Rachel, and not only for the sex either, he flat out missed talking to her. Seeing her in the yard with her camera had become a highlight of his day. Watching her and Alyssa ride out on the horses made him smile.

Dear God, when had he become such a sap? It had snuck up on him, but this last week had proven that it was here to stay, this sappy mush he'd turned into. At least here to stay until she left for good in a month or maybe six weeks. He was going to have to get over this bullshit then, that was for damn sure.

He moved over to look out the window of the office library, the one that faced the drive. No sign of them yet, and he couldn't just stand around watching an empty driveway, for what could be hours.

Beau walked in the door and Adam jerked around trying

to act like he hadn't been mooning, watching the empty driveway. But Beau didn't seem to even notice him, he just walked over and started staring at the driveway, too. A few minutes later their father joined them. None of them said a word, just stood there looking out the window.

After about fifteen minutes his dad sighed. "I really should get to work. There's a lot to be done." But he didn't move from his spot by the window.

Beau nodded. "Yep, same here. Daylight's burning." Beau stayed rooted where he was also.

Finally, Adam said, "We are a sad lot."

Both Beau and Travis looked at him. "What? It's not my fault the women sucked all the joy out of the house by leaving."

Beau gave him a small smile. "You've been keeping your relationship with Rachel on the downlow."

"She'll be leaving in a month to six weeks. Whenever she gets the pics taken you've asked her to take after the wedding. No reason to broadcast something that's not going to remain." Adam shrugged.

His dad lifted an eyebrow. "I've never known you to give up so easily, Son."

He folded his arms. "She's planning to go to art school."

Beau shook his head. "No, she's thinking about going to art school. According to Alyssa she hasn't made up her mind about that."

"And I recall her talking about the old photo studio in town and how much fun she'd have with it." Travis added.

Adam swore. "I know, but I can't be the one to decide for her. Besides she's too young for me."

Beau rolled his eyes and Travis laughed. "Adam, that's one of the dumbest things you've ever said. I married your mother when she was eighteen, I'm six years older than she is. Your grandfather was even more of a cradle robber. He married your grandmother when she was only seventeen, they were seven years apart in age. Rachel is twenty-two and a mature adult. You're the ripe old age of thirty-one. Nothing wrong with that age gap."

Adam frowned. "But if we were still in school—"

Beau whacked him on the back of his head. "You're not still in school, dumbass. Get over it already. There are people out there getting married with a twenty or even thirty-year gap in ages. Less than a decade is nothing. Lighten up."

"Fine, but I still don't think it's my place to decide for Rachel to not go to school." Adam crossed his arms again. He'd never thought about age gaps in his parents or grandparents.

"No one said you have to decide for her," Beau said, "but you might want to offer her some choices."

"I'll think about it." Adam noticed movement out of the corner of his eye. "But right now, it looks like the women are finally home."

Beau and his dad turned their heads so quickly back to the window there was practically a breeze.

"Thank God," Travis said.

"Whoo hoo, last one out the door is a rotten egg," Beau cried and nearly ran out the door, with his father right behind him.

Adam frowned at the discussion as he followed the other two men out of the house. *Am I really being a dumb ass?* Based on the revelations he'd just heard it was no wonder no one else thought a thing about Beau marrying Alyssa.

RACHEL WAS SHOCKED at the feeling of returning home she had when they turned into the driveway of the Rockin' K ranch. She had not felt this feeling of homecoming when she'd arrived in Chedwick or even her family's home a week ago. Her childhood bedroom had seemed foreign to her, even though she'd been living in the room her whole life, up until a couple of months ago.

It was very disconcerting, and she supposed it had something to do with the tall cowboy following his father and brother out the door of the house with a slight frown on his face. That expression changed to a smile when she climbed out of the back seat. It surprised the hell out of her when he came straight to her and wrapped her in a hug. They had never had any PDA in front of his family. Not that anyone was paying attention, since Travis was greeting Meg with a much more enthusiastic greeting. And Alyssa and Beau were devouring each other. Emma was busy releasing her tired little boy from his car seat.

Adam sighed and stepped back. He looked into her eyes. "I missed you."

She felt her smile wobble. "I missed you too. Join me tonight, after dinner?"

His eyes lit. "Happy to. Now let's get this car unloaded." Turning away from her he said, "Beau, quit eating Alyssa's face, we need to get the car emptied."

Beau gave Alyssa one last long kiss then pulled away. "If we must."

Even though the car was packed to the roof with luggage and wedding gifts, it didn't take them long to unload it, especially when the twins and Grandpa K showed up to help.

Rachel went into her room and sank down on the bed. She needed to unpack, download her pictures from the trip, the wedding shower, bachelorette party, and the dress fittings. It had been a long couple of days, so she just wanted to sit for a minute. She looked at her desk and wished she had brought her computer. She'd debated bringing it with her the whole time she was home. In the end, she had left it because Alyssa's wedding gifts had filled the car. Half of them were still in Washington and her family planned to bring them along when they came back for the wedding in three weeks.

She couldn't believe it was only three weeks until the wedding. When she'd first come to Colorado, the few months she would be here seemed like a long time. Now with the end quickly approaching, she wished the time had not gone by so quickly. She would spend a week or two after the wedding getting the pictures taken of the Kipling herd, but then she would be either going back to Washington or off to college.

Her mother had given her the two acceptance letters to the schools she could attend in the fall. She dug the letters out of her purse and looked at them again. They wanted an answer right away, but she didn't know how she wanted to reply. She'd applied late and hadn't really expected acceptance, she was behind in the process and thought they might accept her for the winter term. But both the art school in California and Seattle had accepted her for the fall term, only eight weeks from now. She had the money set aside for the first year, so finances were not an issue and both campuses assured her there was housing available.

She flopped back on her bed and the letters drifted to the floor. She really did not know what she wanted to do. At least that's what she told herself, she was afraid what she really wanted was to stay here in Colorado with grumpy Adam and reopen the photography studio in town. But was that even an option? Yes, he'd said he missed her but that didn't necessarily mean he wanted her to stay either.

Maybe she should just enroll in one of them and move forward, mooning about some guy wasn't smart. But which one should she choose? California would be fun, but she would be very far away from everyone. Seattle was a couple of hours from her family and Sandy, her old babysitter, lived there, so she would know someone.

She got up to get busy. Laying on her bed was not helping in the least. She folded the letters and put them in the night stand to think about later.

CHAPTER 25

Adam was attempting to shave. It was taking forever. He never had minded having a thick beard until recently. When he felt he had to shave all the damn time. He didn't want to give Rachel whisker burn so he'd been shaving at least twice a day to keep from scratching her all up. He'd tackled the chore twice already today, this was his third time.

It was getting ridiculous, he probably could have skipped this morning, but his beard grew so fast that it was habit to clean it up in the morning. Then he'd also done it after lunch, so he didn't look scruffy when the women got home from their trip. The reason he was carefully stripping his chin from whiskers for the third time was because Rachel had invited him to her room and he wanted his face free of anything that might harm her delicate skin. Because he planned to have his lips on every inch of her body.

Thinking about her delicate skin and where his lips would be, was not making his task easier. When he was finally finished, and his face was smooth he rubbed some lotion into his skin to make it a little softer. His face was weathered and rough from spending so much time outdoors.

He grumped about always being indoor away from the sun, but he apparently spent enough time outside to give him a rancher's roughness.

He startled when he walked into his room and found Rachel standing there. "Hi, I thought I was joining you."

"I didn't want to wait." She looked so darn cute in her ratty jeans and T-shirt. He'd come to recognize this particular outfit as her comfort clothes. A slow smile slid across his face. *She didn't want to wait?* So, it wasn't just him feeling eager.

"That's the best news I've heard all week. Maybe even all month."

She rolled her eyes. "Well then don't just stand there, cowboy, make me feel welcome."

He took two long steps to her and pulled her into his arms. She grabbed his hair and pulled his head down, fastened her lips on his and squirmed to get closer. This was not going to be a slow seduction. This was going to be fast and furious if her actions were any indication. And that was fine by him.

She pulled at his T-shirt, so he yanked it over his head. She did the same to her top and he realized she didn't have a bra on. She ran her hands over his chest and then around to the back and pulled him in close, so nothing was between them, not even air.

Her soft breasts molded to his hard chest and it felt like heaven. He devoured her mouth. Lips and tongue and teeth melding, fighting and sometimes crashing together in the rush to consume, to taste, to ravish.

When they had to come up for air she shoved him back and fumbled with his belt, he pushed her bumbling hands away and quickly divested himself of his jeans and shorts. She did the same and they were soon naked. Thank God, he'd put the condoms in his pocket, he didn't think they were going to make it the four steps to the bed. She snatched one and had him sheathed so quickly he barely had time to drop the others.

He hoisted her up and she wrapped her legs around him. He propelled her back against the wall and impaled her in one swift movement. She was plenty ready for him and moaned her pleasure. He tried to slow down, but she wasn't having it.

She gripped his hair. "Fast and hard, Adam. Make me feel it." Then she latched onto his mouth, sucking on his tongue.

He obliged the lady and slammed into her, again and again, until he felt her gather for release. He sped up and gave a little twist of his hips at the end of each stroke and she exploded in his arms. She pulled on his hair and he was sure there would be two bald spots. But then he felt his own self readying, stroked into her a few more times and came hard.

He had her back up against the wall and he was panting, trying to suck in some air. Hopefully his legs wouldn't give out before he regained his strength, dropping her would not be appreciated.

RACHEL REVELED in the fast and furious coupling, Adam was such a slow moving considerate lover, she always felt well taken care of sexually with him. But this time had been off the freakin' charts. So, caveman-ish up against the wall. Like he couldn't wait either, it was glorious.

She put her head on his shoulder and sighed with contentment. "Perfect."

He chuckled. "Glad I could be of assistance. I'll try not to drop you on the way to the bed."

"I could walk. Maybe."

"I think I can manage the four steps," he growled in her ear.

"I don't want you to use all your strength, I have more plans for you." She felt him twitch inside her at the sassy words. She reveled in her feminine ability to rev him up.

"No problem, lovely lady. I can manage both."

He didn't pull out of her as he walked her over to the bed. It was a very odd sensation and kind of arousing. When he got to the bed he lifted her off him and set her down on the bed. After dropping the condom in the trash, he joined her under the covers and pulled her close.

God, she was going to miss this when she went off to college. Refusing to think about that, she snuggled in closer, breathing in his scent. She still had weeks to enjoy the man and she wasn't going to let regrets ruin it.

CHAPTER 26

The wedding went off without a hitch. The dresses turned out beautiful. Barbara had come in a week early to check fit and length. She had each one of them try on their dresses with the shoes they would be wearing at the wedding, so the lengths would be perfect.

Alyssa's dress was simple elegance with seed pearls lining the bodice and hem. She wore white cowboy boots her father had made her. He'd started on them the day after Beau had proposed to her on the video chat. He'd given them to her after everyone had cleared out after the wedding shower. Alyssa had burst into tears and clung onto her father, until his shirt was wet.

Tony and Jill had been adorable. Jill took after her father and had blond hair, but it had the curl of Barbara's and she'd ended up with hazel eyes. Tony had the Kipling dark hair and brown eyes. They looked so cute together. Alyssa's favorite colors were the warm tones of red, yellow and orange. So, Rachel was in red, Emma was in orange and little Jill was in yellow. The men all wore black western style suits with bolo ties and cowboy boots.

Rachel had reigned in her need to be behind the camera, but had kept her eye on the two photographers Alyssa had hired, to make sure they didn't miss anything. She had to admit it looked like they were doing a very good job. They had shown Alyssa and Rachel some of the shots right from the camera, and they looked great. So, Rachel finally relaxed and let them do their job and she did hers as the maid of honor.

She was happy her mom and dad had come to the wedding, she missed them, but she also realized it was time to cut the apron strings and told them she planned to register for college in California. She still wasn't positive she wanted to go to college, but she decided that going back to live in her childhood bedroom was no longer an option. When she told her mom and dad they had looked at each other. Then they had turned to her and told her they were proud of her. They would miss her, but also had realized it was time for her to live away from them. It had been emotional but in a happy way.

Adam had given an excellent toast that had everyone laughing and also pulled a tear or two from most of the ladies. Both dads had given moving toasts and Grandpa K had kept it short and sweet with, "Welcome to the family Alyssa, I'm happy to have a new granddaughter and looking forward to a few more great-grandkids, now let's get to dancing."

Rachel danced with all the Kipling men, including Grandpa K. They were all good dancers, but she enjoyed dancing with Adam the most. She'd also been dragged into dances with half her home town men, and some she didn't know at all, from Colorado. It was fun, and she didn't mind, but a few more dances with Adam would have been even better.

She was a little surprised when he didn't dance with any

of the local women, or any of the single women from Chelan. He only partnered with Rachel, Emma and his mother. She wondered if he didn't like dancing, or what. He was a good dancer, so it wasn't a skill issue. She planned to ask him about that, the next time they were alone.

~

ADAM STOOD at the side of the dance floor and tried not to watch Rachel as every single man in the room danced with her. He was determined not to be jealous. He kept reminding himself, she was too young. She was leaving. He needed a more mature partner, he had responsibilities. But it wasn't working, with each new man she danced with he felt himself tense. There were men from her home town like Tim Jefferson for example. He danced with Rachel, but only once and then he went off to dance with every other female in the room including Adam's mother and the twin's best friend Katie. In fact, if he wasn't mistaken Tim had danced with Katie a couple of times. Well, better than Rachel, in his opinion, anyway.

All of a sudden, the object of his musings was standing in front of him, barefoot and breathing hard. Her hair had come loose from the fancy doodad she'd had it in at the wedding, and there were bits of it hanging down, caressing her bare shoulders. Her skin was flushed and a little damp and he wanted to drag her into the nearest dark corner, push up that fire engine red dress and have his way with her.

She looked at him with sparkling eyes. "Are you going to stand here holding up the wall all night? I could use a reprieve from all these guys I don't know."

"You looked to be holding your own with all of them. And I'm pretty sure you know at least some of them or we have party crashers, because I don't know all of them."

She laughed, a bright sparkling sound. "Yes, I do know some of them. I've danced with everyone and I have been the perfect hostess, but now I just want a break."

"And I'm your break?" he asked lifting his brows at her.

She nodded. "Yes, I know you. In more ways than anyone else in this room, well except for... never mind, old news, not important. With you I can relax. So, come on, give the girl a break and dance with me."

He wondered which guy was the "old news" but maybe it was better he didn't know. So, he didn't have to kill the guy. He sighed deeply, and she laughed again. "If I must."

"Yay."

Even though he had pretended he was doing her a favor, he was delighted to be holding her. He wasn't a bit sad that the music had turned slower, so he could hold her in his arms. He held her close and breathed in her scent as he twirled her on the floor. It seemed to him that everyone had paired back up for this dance. His mom and dad, Rachel's mom and dad, Alyssa's parents, Alyssa and Beau and other married couples or long-time partners. Surprisingly enough Chase was with Katie and Tim was with his little sister Beth.

He whirled Rachel through the next few steps making her laugh. He noticed that the old lady Mrs. Erickson was finally sitting this one out, she'd been out for over half of the dances and she had to be pushing ninety. Her escort, a guy named Greg, was dancing with the woman named Sandy who had developed the *Adventures with Tsilly* game, that everyone loved. Sandy had been as popular on the dance floor as Rachel, but Adam was certain every one of her dance partners had grilled her about the secrets in the most recent release of the game, and questions about what would be in the next one. It didn't look like Greg was grilling Sandy, just holding her close, probably giving her a break, like he was with Rachel.

The longer they danced the more relaxed he became, he wasn't in a hurry for the song to end. He wondered if this might be the last dance of the night. It had to be getting close to the end of the festivities. Beau and Alyssa had commandeered the wedding cabin at the Singing River Ranch for the next two nights, so they could see off their company before flying to Hawaii for ten days. Everyone planned to meet back here tomorrow after lunch, to clean up the Grange. Then his family was going to host everyone for an evening barbeque at the ranch, before all the Washington people left the following morning.

He and Rachel would drive Beau and Alyssa to their honeymoon cabin. There was already a car there and the clothes they would need for the next two days and of course their luggage was all packed up ready for Hawaii. Beau hadn't told anyone which island they were going to, it was a big secret. He didn't think Alyssa even knew.

Rachel snuggled closer and he wondered if she would like to share a bed with him tonight. Maybe not, it had been a long day and she was probably tired. But the way she was pressing up against him, he had to wonder. Time would tell, the woman wasn't shy about letting him know she was interested. He never had to guess.

The song ended and Hank Jefferson walked up to the front where the microphone was. "Thanks for coming folks. That's the last of the festivities for the evening. Please join us outside to see the bride and groom off."

The kids with their bubbles raced for the door. Adam signaled Beau to indicate he'd have the transportation at the end of the tunnel of friends. Then he and Rachel went out to drive the carriage up. They'd thought about riding horses away from the event, but had decided that horse drawn carriage would be fun. One of their neighbors was a history buff and had two different ones that he gave people rides with during the peak tourist times. He'd loaned them the smaller one for the wedding. They were only going a couple of miles so it would be a fun sight. He'd assigned the decorating of the carriage to the twin sets and it looked great.

He helped Rachel up into the driver's seat and clambered up next to her.

"The twins did a great job, the decorations are perfect, not too few and not too gaudy," she said.

He nodded. "I was thinking the same thing. I think any tourists in town are going to get a kick out of it."

"I wonder if anyone from Chedwick will get a wild hair to add it to one of the wedding destination packages offered in town."

Adam looked at her as he started the horses to walking toward the front of the building. "Your town had destination weddings?"

"Yes, it was one of the ideas that was suggested at a town meeting a few years ago to draw more tourists. There were three ideas actually." She ticked them off on her fingers as she told him. "The first was to capitalize on the popularity of the *Adventures with Tsilly* game, which spawned an amusement park. The second was to showcase the many artisans that live in our town, which culminated in a new website and an eclectic art gallery, that has my photos, Tim's wood carvings, and a whole bunch of other local artists. The crowning work is Lucille Thompson's glass art. The third is destination weddings."

"Even I have heard of Lucille Thompson. How did she get involved?"

"It's a bit of a long story for this moment. But the short version is her son, Nolan, became our town sheriff, so she brought her art when Kristen opened the gallery."

Adam nodded. "Interesting. Here they come. You'll have to tell me the long version someday."

"Will do. I hope all those bubbles don't scare the horses."

"No worries."

Adam held the horses still while Beau and Alyssa ran the gauntlet of friends and then scrambled into the carriage.

The crowd started chanting. "Kiss, kiss." So, Beau and Alyssa obliged them as Adam started the horses to walking. Some of the teenagers chased after them continuing the chant. Tourists and shop workers came out to continue the chant as he walked the horses down main street.

CHAPTER 27

Once they finally got all the Chedwick people on their way home and the bridal couple driving to Denver to catch a plane to Hawaii, Rachel knew she could finally work on photographing the cattle. It was her last project in Colorado. On one hand she was excited to do the documentation and since Alyssa was gone she would have time to do a little more exploring. On the other hand, she thought she might be sad to be leaving soon.

There were a lot of places she wanted to visit with her camera, she'd been in Colorado for months and had barely gotten off the ranch. There had been plenty to photograph on the ranch, it had some very pretty areas. But she wanted to go a bit further afield before she left.

Adam planned to get his work done in the morning and then meet up with her after lunch to work on the cattle. That gave her plenty of time to do some exploring and in great light, too. Morning or late afternoon light were the best. Adam had also said he would take her to some places that were his favorite on the weekends.

They'd decided it would take two weeks to get all the

herd documented. Which meant she'd also be there when Beau and Alyssa got back. So, she could hear about their grand adventures in Hawaii.

Her first morning she decided to get up early and drive toward the National Park to see what might be feeding in the clearing Adam had shown her. She left before dawn, it was about a half hour drive, so she should hit the meadow right as the sun was coming up, which was good because she wasn't sure she could find it without some daylight. There were no street lights along that stretch of road, at least not many.

She took a bottle of water and a thermos of coffee with her, glad someone had made the morning kickstart. There were some granola bars and a big bowl of peaches. She'd heard that the western slope of the Colorado Rockies had delicious peaches, but she hadn't tried one yet. She washed the peach and wrapped it in some paper towels, she noticed it had a heavenly smell that made her want to eat it immediately, but she wanted to get on the road. Gathering up all her snacks she put them in a backpack, slung that over one shoulder and the camera bag over another. She carried her coffee out to the Silver Bullet and climbed in.

She drove toward the National Park entrance. There was only one main road, so it wasn't hard to find. The sun was just barely starting to rise when she saw meadow where she'd seen the mule deer the first time. Nothing was moving about and since it was too dark to take any pictures she decided to eat the peach since she could still smell it.

Parked on the side of the road she pulled it out of the bag and it filled the whole car with the sweet smell of peaches. She took a bite and the taste exploded on her tongue, it was sweet and so juicy it dribbled down her chin. She grabbed up the paper towels and wrapped it around the peach to catch the extra juice, although she didn't want to waste a drop. She slurped the juice as she took another bite. The pulp was the perfect consistency, not too mushy, not too woody, just perfect. She reveled in the taste and although some of the juice was lost to the paper towel and her hands it was the most delicious peach she'd ever eaten. She decided that the people who raved about the Colorado peaches were geniuses.

When she was finished with her sticky snack she found some hand wipes in the back pack and cleaned herself up as much as possible, just as something walked into the clearing. It was pretty far away, on the far side of the meadow, but looked really big. She grabbed up her camera and used the telephoto lens to zoom in on it. Gasping she waited while it lowered its head to eat. When its head raised again she was certain it was a moose. It was too big to be a deer and it was not quite shaped right either. She'd never seen a moose before, but it sure looked like she was seeing one today. She took a few pictures, but it was still so dark, and it was so far away she didn't get very good pictures.

If only he would move closer. She quickly put aside the idea of crossing the field. Not knowing what the ground was like under all the grass would make traipsing across the field foolish. A Moose could be dangerous if he felt threatened and she had no intention of making him feel uncomfortable. As she watched the big guy eating it looked like he was wandering a little closer to her and with the light getting stronger she was able to take a few better pictures.

A small herd of deer also entered the area on the other end of the field from the moose and neither seemed inclined to get closer to the other. She swapped back and forth between taking pictures of the deer herd and the moose.

A car came down the road moving at a fast pace. All of a sudden it slammed on its brakes and backed up halfway onto the shoulder but was still sticking out a bit onto the road. A family of five jumped out of the car yelling about seeing the deer. They started off across the field toward the deer. The moose was not in their direct line of sight because of some trees and Rachel was worried they would agitate it. Both the deer and the moose heard the commotion however and wasted no time leaving the area.

Rachel shook her head at the idiots that some people were, as the family whined about the deer leaving. Then they piled back into their car to take off back down the road. Rachel was disappointed that the idiot family had scared the animals off, but was glad the animals had not waited around. She was fairly certain those were the kind of people who would get too close and then be angry when one of the animals fought back.

She decided to take a few more pictures of the meadow and then start back towards the Rockin' K taking pictures as her whim dictated.

ADAM WAS FINISHING up his work for the morning. He'd added in some of tomorrow's work also thinking maybe he could get caught up enough to take a week day off to spend with Rachel. He knew he wanted to take her back into the National Park on Saturday to drive her over the Old Fall River Road. And he'd talked to a friend about using his boat to go out on the lakes on Sunday, Grand Lake and Shadow Mountain Lake were connected by a canal, so he thought they could explore both lakes and give her lots of picture taking vistas. If they had a third day they could either rent a boat to visit Lake Granby or he could take her into the National Forest or to Hot Sulphur Springs, although he would have to see if she brought a swim suit if they wanted to get into the springs. There were too many places he wanted to take her and not enough time.

Getting all the cattle photographed was going to eat up the afternoons, but maybe she could get ahead of the game and they could both take an extra day off this week and maybe next week too. He'd have to hustle to do both and so would she. Although with the days being longer they could easily work a little later in the evening.

He was kind of surprised he was so excited about playing tour guide and helping her with the cattle. One of his brothers could help her with the cattle, but he felt reluctant to ask them, he found himself anticipating the time with her.

She walked into the office as he finished paying the bills for this week, he grinned at her eagerness. They had planned to meet after lunch which wasn't for a half hour, guess he wasn't the only one anticipating.

"I came back early because I thought you could show me your website and what you might want to enhance. Or some of the pictures other people take to sell cattle online. Plus, some dumbass people chased away the deer and moose I was taking pictures of."

Instant fear coursed through his veins at the thought of her encountering a moose. He looked up sharply. "You didn't—"

She cut him off. "No, I did not go near the animals I was very happy staying next to my car and zooming in on them. But another car came along with a family and they were shouting and started off toward the deer which turned tail and bounded off. They didn't even see the moose, but he was no fool either and took off."

Relieved that she had been smart about the encounter, he shook his head. "Some people are idiots."

"Yes, they are. So, show me your website."

He nodded and turned back to the computer. "We have a

web site for our ranch. A lot of ranches don't. They register with a kind of *cattle clearing house* that lists how many of which bulls or heifers they want to sell. They list them by breed and other qualifications."

He clicked on a clearing house, so she could see what he was talking about. "This one is just lists of animals, but this one has pictures of each animal for sale."

She nodded. "Yes, the one with the pictures looks better to me but that's my own prejudice showing."

He grinned. "We used to use one of those, but then we decided to create our own website. It's been nice having our own, because people don't have to wade through as much information, if they want stock specifically from our ranch. We have a good reputation."

He typed in their web address, so their page came up. "So far, we've just listed what cattle are available, but if we put the pictures of the available animals up it would be even better. See it's just a list, unlike that one clearing house that had small pictures of each animal."

"It's a nice site, the picture of the Rocky Mountains with some of the cattle grazing in the foreground is a nice touch. But you're right when it gets to the animal selection it could use more graphics. Right now, it's utilitarian, but it could be nicer."

"Exactly. So, if we had you take pictures of the ones we want to sell, plus the ones Beau wants to put in his presentation that would be a great start."

Rachel said, "Beau also talked about putting a picture of each one into a database."

"The birthing records. Yeah that would be nice, it would make it harder to get the cattle mixed up. One of the hired hands has dyslexia, I think Beau was thinking it might help with that. But it's not as important. I'm not sure we could photograph the entire herd in the two weeks you have left."

She looked at him intently for a few moments and he had to wonder what she was thinking. But then she shrugged, and the moment passed. "Well let's get started, daylight's burning." She sent him a sassy grin.

"So, you've picked up on the favorite family saying I see." He said with a groan.

"It is an excellent saying."

"Just don't tell Grandpa K you think so."

"Too late. I already did."

He groaned again more dramatically. "Tell me it isn't true. He's already bad enough."

She laughed, and he shivered, as the musical sound vibrated on the air and through his whole body. He swatted her playfully on the ass. "Bad girl, let's get some lunch."

He picked up the list Beau had left, of which cattle he needed for his artificial insemination talk at the college. And there was also the list Adam and his father had made of cattle they wanted to sell. They could start on those and then see if there was going to time to photograph the entire herd.

During lunch Rachel made it clear she thought that plan of attack was silly.

She frowned at him. "If we might need to photograph all of them, why don't we just take a picture of each one we come upon, rather than drive all over the ranch looking for the "special" ones and then have to go back a second time for the rest."

"But what if we can't get through the whole herd in two weeks and then miss some of the ones we need pictures of?"

"Well if my idea isn't working we can always switch to your idea. The herd is not quite one thousand, right? If we only work the weekdays that's one hundred per day in five hours that would be twenty per hour, but the sun goes down about eight so even with an hour off for dinner we could put in seven hours, that's only fifteen per hour. When they are all together in one area that will be easy. I can set up my camera and you can bring them in front of it. Or if that doesn't work I'll just walk around and take their pictures."

He nodded. "I see, so we keep track of how many you take each day and if we keep on track with roughly one hundred a day we'll be good. We can check off the critical ones at night."

"Yeah, exactly. You can record the order we take them in. So, we can match the image with the animal name."

"Number, the animals have numbers, not names."

"Oh, how sad, they don't get a name. Poor nameless animals. How come Dolly has a name then?"

She looked so disheartened when he told her the story of Dolly he tried to think of every funny story he knew so it would cheer her up. He was rewarded for his efforts with several laughing bouts.

CHAPTER 28

Rachel was having such a good time working with Adam, she didn't want this time to end, but it was speeding by. Adam had a dry sense of humor that she loved. In the beginning it had taken her a minute to realize he was joking, but she'd finally caught on and now he cracked her up on a regular basis. They had taken pictures of so many cows she was certain she was going to see them in her dreams for years. But she'd learned a lot about them and now could tell the difference in the breeds as well as the ages with just a glance.

They had taken three days off to go play in the vicinity. Adam had kept her to a fast schedule the first three days, telling her if they got enough done they could take Thursday off to go exploring. They'd managed it with longer days but it had been worth every second. Each day he had a different adventure planned.

Since they managed to take Thursday off, Adam suggested they go into the Rocky Mountain National Park that day because there would be less tourists and therefore less traffic. She agreed so they started the drive over Trail

Ridge road this time heading toward Estes Park. He wanted to take her over the Old Fall River road which was one way and started on the Estes Park side of the park.

Adam said, "We can stop at most of the same turnouts we did the first time, since it's later in the summer the flowers will be in full bloom."

"Goody." Rachel said, "This direction is a little more harrowing feeling, since we're next to the downhill side."

"Yes, it is, but don't worry we'll be fine." Adam patted her knee.

"I'm sure we will be as long as you pay attention."

He grinned. "Yes ma'am."

"We'll have to stop and see how my little bud is doing."

"We can do that, what you did with those pictures was fascinating. I thought you'd lost your mind while you were taking them, but you really know what you're doing."

"Well thank you, kind sir." He turned off the road. "That is a beautiful profusion of flowers. Thanks for stopping."

"Of course. That is the point of this trip to let you take lots of pictures."

She nodded. "And have some fun at the same time."

"Fun and a picnic. There is a waterfall on the dirt road, we can have our picnic by that."

"Great." She got out of the car and took lots of pictures of the sturdy little flowers growing in the harsh climate. She knew this time to bring a jacket for the drive. Even though it was warmer than it had been, the wind at this elevation was still cold.

As they walked back to Adam's truck an SUV tooted their horn and Adam waved.

Rachel watched the car drive on. "The passenger had a sweater over her head. I assume it was a her since it was a female type of sweater."

Adam laughed. "Yes, that was Ruth Williamson, she's

terrified of Trail Ridge road. Her husband loves it. So once a year they take it into Estes Park and spend the day shopping and playing tourist and then drive back. She pretty much spends the whole drive with a sweater over her head, so she can't see the drop-offs."

She looked towards where the truck had disappeared from view. "And they've been doing this for how long?"

"They've probably been married going on forty years."

"And she's still terrified?" she asked.

"Yep."

"People are weird."

"Yep."

She laughed as they got in the car to continue the drive. Rachel thought about the old couple, how the woman would sacrifice her fear of the road, so her husband could drive on the road he loved. She wondered how many times he wanted to drive it and sacrificed his joy for his wife's fears. Love really was about give and take and those two exemplified it.

She knew Adam enjoyed driving but she wondered if he had things he would rather be doing. Not that he was doing it out of love, but still she wondered.

ADAM ENJOYED TAKING Rachel around to the different places he had lined up for her. They'd had a good day in the national park, she'd loved the Old Fall River road and they'd had a fun picnic near the falls. Fortunately, there was only one other car they saw on the road, since it was a Thursday. So, they pretty much had the road to themselves and could just stop in the middle of it whenever she wanted to take a photo or two.

They'd gone out on the lakes in his friend's boat on Saturday and they'd had a lot of fun doing that. She took a ton of pictures and then he let her drive the boat for a while. She'd learned how to pilot a boat in her home town on Lake Chelan but hadn't gotten to do it a lot. It had been a fun day with lots of laughs. Fortunately, they'd slathered on sunscreen so they didn't get burnt.

Sunday, they decided was going to be a chill day. She took her camera with her, but said it was not going to be the focus of the day. They took the drive to Hot Sulphur Springs and she'd taken a lot of pictures on the drive and then some of the town, but when they were ready to go in to the actual pools she'd locked her camera up in his truck and they walked into the springs hand in hand.

She'd about given him a heart attack when she shimmied out of her jeans and had on her skimpy bathing suit. It wasn't nearly as tiny as some he'd seen, but it fit her so well he knew he started drooling.

She smiled a naughty smile. "I'm glad I brought my suit. I almost didn't, not knowing if it would be warm enough to warrant it. But I was planning to be here for most of the summer, so I decided to drag it along. It doesn't take much room anyway."

He had to swallow twice to get his throat to work. "I'm glad you brought it too. And no, it wouldn't take much room. What it did take is so worth it. I need a picture of that if you don't mind. I can take it on my phone."

She posed and laughed. "If you must."

He took several as she grinned and posed for the shots. Then it was her turn to take pictures of him with her phone, so he clowned around like she had. He didn't know how she felt about his pictures, but he was fairly certain the shots of her were going to become a prized possession.

They'd had dinner in a quaint restaurant, she'd brought a sexy sun dress to wear after the hot springs and he'd cleaned up some also. The restaurant had a bar with a dance floor and live music, so they danced and acted like they were on a date. Rather than him being a tour guide. He'd liked it, he'd liked it a lot.

That night she'd joined him in his room and they'd made slow passionate love to one another. It was a special day and one he would remember for a very long time.

CHAPTER 29

Alyssa and Beau were due back tonight. Rachel would be happy to see her friend and hear about her Hawaiian adventures. But Rachel's time on the ranch was coming to an end too quickly. In less than a week she would be on the road headed to California to make her final arrangements to start school. She needed an apartment and to pay her tuition and buy books and look over the campus. She would be a freshman, so the course schedule was pretty standard, at least until she could see what she should test out of. Not much to do about that right away though.

After she got everything arranged she'd need to make a trip back to Washington to collect whatever she would need to spend the next four years in college. She planned to fly up, then rent a small truck to bring back down whatever she would need, depending on what she got as living quarters and whether they were furnished.

It was a lot to do, but frankly she was not looking forward to it. In some ways she knew the experience would be valuable and she would learn a lot, but her heart wasn't in it.

She'd lost her heart right here in the Colorado mountains to a man she would never have chosen. He wasn't at all the kind of guy she normally dated or was interested in. But her heart had a mind of its own.

He never talked about her staying. He managed their time, so she would have everything done in the time that was allotted. She wondered if he would be glad to be rid of her. Or if he was biding his time until she packed up and moved on.

She laughed. *Cynical much?* Just then he walked out of the house and grinned when he saw her.

"I hurried with my work, so, we could get stuff done before the newlyweds show up and distract us."

"That's probably a good idea. I'm excited to hear about their time in Hawaii. Someday I want to go, there is so much beautiful photography from the islands, but I would still want to take my own."

"You would have a different slant on it and bring your own flavor. I will be watching for your famous photography from now on. Someday you'll be a headliner, for sure."

She felt her heart swell with his pride in her, while at the same time wished she wasn't going anywhere. Did she really want to be a famous photographer? She didn't know if she did. "Well thanks for your confidence, but I'm not sure I'm the famous type. I'm happy to be in the background taking pictures. Someone else can have the limelight."

"When you do become famous, you can set your own standards and be eccentric. Refuse all the attention. Brush off reporters with a comment on how you lose your creativity when you give pieces of yourself away in interviews."

She rolled her eyes. "You are so silly. Let's get moving, we're burning daylight."

He rolled his eyes back at her. "Grandpa K has created a monster."

~

ADAM WAS HAVING fun teasing her and it was keeping him from being depressed about her leaving at the end of the week. He was going to miss the woman. What he wanted to do, was to beg her to stay and marry him. He would love to take her to Hawaii and anywhere else she wanted to travel. He would happily become her pack mule for life. But he couldn't derail her career.

She had so much potential and he meant it when he said he would be waiting and watching for her to become a top photographer. The work she'd shown him was amazing, and here he had her out photographing a bunch of animals any idiot could take pictures of. Nope, he wasn't going to let on that he wanted her to stay with him. He was going to work with her up until the last day, then he was going to smile and wave as she drove her little silver car out of his life.

He couldn't bear to think about that, so getting busy with work was the cure. They still had a couple hundred head of cattle to photograph. They would have to spend the last day hunting down all the ones that had been missed. He'd been thinking about a strategy for that. Maybe have everyone that was available spread out across the ranch and look for the missing ones. When they found the correct animals, they could text in their location and keep the cattle from moving until Rachel could drive around to the different locations.

They spent the day as they had many others, chatting as they took all the pictures they could before dinner. When they got back to the house Beau and Alyssa had arrived.

At dinner the newlyweds talked about Hawaii.

Rachel gasped. "You did not go all the way to Hawaii and spend half your time on cattle ranches. Please tell me I misunderstood that."

Alyssa laughed at her best friend. "Nope, you understood

perfectly. We went to the Big Island and it has one of the largest cattle ranches in Hawaii and very historic too. There were some up north and others down south. We had a great time."

"But you were supposed to be swimming in the ocean and soaking up the rays and having sex. Not working." Rachel whined.

"We did plenty of those things, too. And it wasn't work exactly, it was interesting to see how they handle it on such a closed environment. We loved it, didn't we honey?" Alyssa looked at Beau.

He nodded. "We did, indeed."

Alyssa shook her finger at Rachel. "Besides, missy, if it was you on your honeymoon, you can't tell me you wouldn't have your camera out taking a zillion pictures." Adam had to admit Alyssa had a point, Rachel would have that camera strapped to her hand the entire time.

Rachel huffed. "That's different. Everyone takes pictures."

"It's not different at all. The ranch we went to has a visitor's center and a lot of people go to it as tourists." Alyssa shrugged. "We just asked different questions, and spent a bit more time there."

"Fine. But I still think it was silly to go thousands of miles away and end up on a ranch." Rachel folded her arms and Adam had to hold in the chuckle he felt as the two women argued. They were so darn funny together.

"Changing the subject." Alyssa grinned. "So, you leave this weekend for college. I'll help you with the last few days of picture taking so we can spend the time together. Okay?"

Adam felt his enjoyment plummet. He didn't want Alyssa to push him out of his last few days with Rachel.

Rachel looked at him. "But Adam and I have a system down."

Alyssa laughed. "And I can't figure it out? I'm sure he's got plenty of work to do since you've been taking up half his time."

Adam shook his head. "Actually, I've been able to keep up just fine. I simply start a little earlier in the morning."

"Well now you can go back to your regular schedule," Alyssa said.

"If you insist." He didn't know what else to say and maybe Rachel would prefer to spend the last couple of days with her best friend. She didn't argue with the plan, so maybe she was tired of him.

"I do. It will be fun." Alyssa grinned at Rachel.

Rachel smiled back at her friend and nodded. Although the smile wasn't as enthusiastic as Alyssa's he could see it was genuine. He'd lost, and he'd just have to suck it up. He didn't say much the rest of the evening as Alyssa and Beau continued to share their stories of Hawaii.

CHAPTER 30

Rachel woke up alone. Adam had left. She didn't remember him leaving so he must have done so while she was asleep. He'd loved her last night, over and over, almost frantically. She'd been convinced he was going to ask her to stay. But he was nowhere to be found and there was a note on her bedside table that told her good luck in college and then he'd signed it with "think of me".

Well, so much for a profession of undying love. It clearly wasn't happening. They were obviously not on the same page. She sniffed, she was not going to cry over the man. She was going to pack up her car and drive to California and enroll in school.

The tears in her eyes were tears of joy, not sadness. She refused to cry over a man that wouldn't even see her off, or tell her goodbye. The jerk.

She'd just finished getting dressed when Alyssa knocked on her door.

"I came to help you pack. I'm going to miss you."

"I'm going to miss you, too."

"No, you won't you'll be so busy in college you won't have time to miss me. You're going to have so much fun."

Rachel forced a smile, knowing her friend thought she knew what was best. "I'll still miss you. But I can always stalk you on social media."

"For sure, and you'll have to post some of your work as you learn new stuff. I'll be waiting with bated breath."

Rachel laughed. "I'm sure you will, in between breeding the cattle, and delivering new calves, and sewing up hurt animals, and getting caught in snowstorms."

"I'll still have time to check for new pictures." Alyssa put her hands on her hips. "Now let's get you all loaded up. It's a long drive to California."

They spent the morning packing and filling the car with all Rachel's belongings. Meg brought her out a hamper of food to eat on the journey and the whole family came to say goodbye and wish her luck. All except for Adam, he was nowhere to be seen. After they all said their goodbyes, Rachel got in the car and the family went inside for lunch.

All that was left was to start the car and drive off.

ADAM RODE JAKE back into the yard and saw Rachel's car sitting there still loaded and waiting for her. He groaned, he'd been a chicken-shit and had tried to hide out until she left, but it hadn't worked. She was still here. He hadn't wanted to have to say goodbye. He'd done that last night with his body. Loving her with everything he had. Showing her in every way how much she meant to him. He didn't think he could actually say the words without begging her to stay. But he couldn't do that, she was young, and she deserved to go to college and lead her life, maybe even find a younger man to love.

Grandpa K walked out of the barn and looked at him still sitting on his horse staring at her car. "You owe her a good-bye, even if you aren't brave enough to ask her to stay."

He sighed. "It's not that I'm not brave enough, it's that she deserves the time to find herself."

"Never saw her act like she didn't know exactly who she was, or what she wanted. Are you sure you're not the one that needs to find himself?" Grandpa K said with a lifted brow.

"But her college..."

"Seems to me she never was too excited about going to college. In fact, it seems to me that the idea of opening up that old photo studio in town was the thing that excited her the most. Might just be she's waiting for an invitation to make this her home." He shrugged. "But I'm just an old fool, you probably shouldn't listen to me." Then he started walking toward the house.

Adam scoffed at the idea. His grandfather had one of the keenest minds he knew. "Grandpa?"

He didn't turn, just pointed. "She took a horse, went that way."

Adam was certain he knew where she'd gone. His land was that way and she loved that old swing that sat by the river. Adam turned his horse around and urged him into a run. He couldn't get there fast enough.

He breathed a sigh of relief when he saw her horse tethered to a tree. He tied his next to hers and walked toward the river.

She sat cross-legged on the swing with her back to him. She didn't turn as he walked up behind her and knelt on the ground. She looked so damn beautiful in her ragged jeans and white T-shirt.

He whispered, "You're still here."

She nodded, but didn't answer or look at him.

"Why?"

She stared at the river and then shrugged. "I don't want to leave."

She said it so quietly he nearly couldn't hear her. But his heart leapt with joy, maybe he had a chance.

He cleared his throat. "I don't want you to leave either."

She finally turned and looked at him. "You don't?"

"No. I couldn't bear the thought of you leaving, that's why I left this morning while it was still dark. I couldn't watch you drive away. I love you."

"Then I'll stay."

"And marry me?"

She sighed and closed her eyes as a smile curved her lips. "Yes. I'll marry you. I love you too, Adam. So very much."

The End

ABOUT THE AUTHOR

I am a former techy turned writer. I'm writing two small town contemporary romance series with some other ideas percolating in my brain. The Lake Chelan Series is the first series and there are several more books planned for it. The Burlap and Barbed Wire series is a spinoff from the Lake Chelan series. All the books are stand alone but they are also fun to read in order.

I have lived in Colorado, Hawaii, and currently Washington. I'm a member of RWA (Romance Writers of America) and the local chapters GSRWA (Greater Seattle RWA) and Eastside RWA.

My family consists of two grown children, their spouses, two adorable grand-daughters, and one grand dog. I started reading at a young age with the Nancy Drew mysteries and have continued to be an avid reader. My favorite reading material these days is romance in most of the genres.

My favorite activity is playing with my grand-daughters!

Some of the jobs I have held are a carnation grower's worker, a trap club puller, a pizza hut waitress, a software engineer, an international trainer, and a business program manager.

And for something really unusual... I once had a raccoon as a pet.

~

To sign up for Shirley's New Release Newsletter, send email to shirleypenick@outlook.com, Subject: Newsletter.

For more information:
www.shirleypenick.com